To LIV and DIE

IN

EL VALLE

Oscar Mancinas

Arte Público Press
Houston, Texas

To Live and Die in El Valle is made possible through a grant from the National Endowment for the Arts. We are grateful for their support.

Recovering the past, creating the future

Arte Público Press
University of Houston
4902 Gulf Fwy, Bldg 19, Rm 100
Houston, Texas 77204-2004

Cover design by Mora Des!gn

To LIVE and DIE

IN

EL VALLE

To my unborn child

"These [kids], now, were living as we'd been living then, they were growing up with a rush and their heads bumped abruptly against the low ceiling of their actual possibilities."

James Baldwin

Acknowledgements

I'd like to thank these publications which first gave these stories, or versions of them, life:

"Arizona Boy." *Cosmonauts Avenue*, May 2018.
"To Live and Die in EV." *Storm Cellar Quarterly* Vol. 6 No. 2, Fall 2017.
"Suicide Survivor's Guide to What's Next." *Cosmonauts Avenue*, November 2016.
"Tourista." *The Tishman Review* Vol. 2 Issue 4, October 2016.
"Cut & Fade." *3Elements Review* Issue 12, October 2016.
"Falsas Promesas." *Contraposition* Vol. 5, Fall 2015.

I would also like to thank Pablo Medina, Jabari Asim, Katerina González Seligmann, John Trimbur, John Skoyles, Beth Parfitt, Kim McLarin and Maria Koundoura for their mentorship and guidance. Dean Allbritton, Aaron Decker and Carlos Villacorta González for their encouragement and counsel. Stephen Shane, Peter Medeiros, Sally Burnette, Doug Koziol, Simón Jiménez, Joseph Santaella Vidal, Michelle Betters, Erin Jones, John Taylor, Marie Sweetman, Anthony Martínez and Zoë Gadegbeku for their brilliance and their warmth. Lali Balbuena, Laura González Flores, Carter Walker, Jocie Fifield, Tim Corkum, Noah Teachey, Ramón Álvarez, James "Flip" Shaum and Peter & Katie Van Schrampel for their wonderful friendship. Dulce Arámbula for her care, patience, understanding, wisdom and love—*te amo, alma mía.* All my peoples in Washington-Escobedo, East Boston, Lima, Monterrey, Batopilas, Los Mochis, without y'all, I'm nothing—*sin ustedes no soy nada.* Finally, I want to thank *mi amá y mi apá:* María Mercedes Barranca & Óscar Mancinas Martínez. Everything I am and can be is all due to your unbelievable strength, affection, resolve and knowledge. *Los quiero mucho.*

Table of Contents

Comenzamos: Falsas Promesas

What difference did it make? *Después de haber sufrido tanto, nos fuimos.* That's how it started, that's how it kept going. When we lost almost everything, the only option left to live was to leave. So we left. But leaving did not fix everything. We still needed to survive, to provide life. *A trabajar pues.* We worked. We worked our bodies, we worked our land, we worked our sky, we worked. We worked with the promise that come nightfall, the dark desert would soothe our soreness, ease our pain. We worked until we forgot, or tried to forget, what kind of sun would rise tomorrow. *Por lo pronto, ¡nos pusimos a pistear en la pinche pachanga! ¡A romper todo con nuestros gritos, se ha dicho!*

Meanwhile, our little ones sat, watched, learned, remembered. *¿Qué más?* What else?

The night begins like it can never stop, but there's a point in the party where the men say to the women, "I love you. No. I *REALLY* love you." They sound angry, but what do love and anger have to do with each other? *Mamá* and *las tías* act like they don't hear them. They've felt this before: the 2 am summer, the *norteña* pouring from the speakers and collecting on the floor in a sea so big, so deep, no one gets out. They close their eyes, and they face the darkness of the ground or the darkness of the sky. It's been the same darkness their whole lives, even now—even *en el otro lado,* where people pay cash to have their houses all look the same—here, too, the darkness overflows from the cups, the cans and the bottles, and we try to drink it. Drink it all before the adults open their eyes. The lights come on and we're still.

Entradas 2001

I.

"What's your name?"

"Fernanda Eusebia Díaz."

"Where were you born?"

"Eh . . . El Valle, Arizona . . . *en* nigh-tee-ey-tee-nigh."

"Where are you coming from?"

"Sonora . . . Obregón."

"Where are you going?"

"Em . . . with my *mamá* . . . to home."

"Who is the man driving the car for you and your mother?"

"He is . . . Josué. *Mamá's* friend."

The border patrolman said nothing. Instead, he looked down at Fernanda, trying to penetrate her thoughts to reveal her lies. She tried not to make any movements he might read as guilt, but she could feel her body getting lighter and warmer. Just as she felt herself about to cry, another patrolman called to them, interrupting everything.

She looked over and saw Josué laughing with a group of patrolmen. Her mother was bowing nervously, in gratitude, before getting back into Josué's car.

The patrolman who had been questioning Fernanda shoved her fake birth certificate back at her, squinted at her mother and Josué and muttered something she didn't understand.

Fernanda thought about saying "Thank you" the way she knew *gringos* did, but she didn't want to speak anymore English until she was forced to. She took her document, folded it carefully and walked towards the car, self-conscious about her trembling body.

Back on the road, Josué smoked cigarettes, played *corridos* on the radio and laughed.

"I told you it was this easy," he said. "I told you, I told you, I told you."

Flor, Fernanda's mother, whispered eternal gratitude and loyalty to *La Virgencita* and clutched her rosary to her chin as she crossed herself.

Outside the car, the desert fanned by. Fernanda's head swirled. She needed air and felt like there wasn't enough air in the whole world for her anymore. Turning from the window, she looked down and saw the blue LA Dodgers cap she had been given by a family friend before leaving Obregón. She forgot that she had taken it off when they stopped at the border. She reached for it and pulled it down over her eyes. The smell of sweat calmed her a little.

This was how they got to El Valle.

"The girl has to go to school, Flor," Doña Carmen had said on their first night in El Valle. "In this country, a girl of eleven who is not in school draws too much attention."

Fernanda sat in the dark on a mattress that was emanating the smell of other people. Maybe because of the darkness, the conversation outside between the two adult women seemed to funnel directly to the corner of the one-room house where Fernanda sat. The small house, which sat behind Doña Carmen's house on a mostly unlit street, would be their new home for who knew how long. Fernanda could feel her mother's anxiety as she talked with her distant cousin. She did not know if she imagined it or if her mother's voice sounded as fragile as Fernanda's body felt. Even though the weather had been warm and sunny throughout the drive, Fernanda felt a coldness she could not fight. She wished she could be anywhere else but there.

"*Pero*, what . . . what do we say if . . . I don't want to overuse these documents, in case they become suspicious," Flor said.

"*No te preocupes, comadre,*" Doña Carmen said. "They don't ask for much documentation. Just an address and phone number. You can use our information. No problem."

Flor's voice, on the brink of breaking, thanked Doña Carmen over and over again.

* * *

The first day at Roosevelt Middle School felt to Fernanda like crossing the border a million times an hour. She spent the first minutes of each class nodding slowly to whatever the teacher said. Every teacher sighed and shook their head. One even yelled English words at her. Ve. Ry. Slow. Ly. Like. A. Ham. Mer. Hit. Ting. Her. Head. All. Mor. Ning.

Turning to her classmates, Fernanda saw smirks and eye rolls. Some girls whispered about her in Spanish but made no attempt to actually talk to her. Her first relief came in her third class, math, when she could, at least, do all the problems that didn't involve writing, reading or talking. The second relief came during gym class, when she and the other kids were allowed to just run around. At lunch, however, she was again alone.

While she ate the last of the egg and *frijol* tacos her mom had packed her, the bell rang. It was time for her to go back inside the school. From where she sat, she could see an opening in the fence at the far end of a field. Fences and their small openings were all around her, she thought, and she hated it. She closed her eyes and turned up to the bright, March sun. She couldn't possibly go back into the school for more, she thought. She couldn't stay here.

"*Oye*, you're gonna be late if you don't wake up from your *siesta*," a voice said in Spanish, breaking her trance.

Her eyes jolted open. In front of her, a sweaty boy in a purple cap smirked and shook his head. His Spanish reminded Fernanda of how people in Obregón spoke. Before she could say anything, he ran towards the main school building. She got up and followed him.

II.

Sitting on a bench on the other side of the leftfield fence, Fernanda was far enough so they wouldn't see her but close enough to still hear them.

"*Oye oye oye*, Mexican Barry Bonds at the plate. Back up, y'all, back up."

Moments later, a thwack and shouting. A small, off-white ball came rolling through the yellowed grass and gently touched the fence in front her.

Then he came running. In a pair of dusty jeans, a white T-shirt and that same purple cap, the boy she had followed to find this field. He ran and grabbed the ball with his free hand. Before he turned and hurled it back toward the infield, though, his eyes met hers, and he paused. The others yelled as the play went on, but he looked at Fernanda, wearing a white T-shirt, shorts and her ponytail pulled out the back of her Dodger's hat. He smiled.

"Ooh, Nesto, did you bring your girlfriend to cheer for you?" a tall boy called out from home plate. He was the biggest boy Fernanda had ever seen. He rested a bat on his right shoulder; his black curls poked out of a light blue hat with a B on the front.

Ernesto ignored him and walked towards a boy on the pitcher's mound. Fernanda, her arms stiff at her sides, walked behind him. At the mound, Ernesto nodded, and the pitcher called for time. Two other boys, one from first base and one from right field, came jogging to the mound. The only boy who didn't move was the big one at home plate.

Outside the huddle, Fernanda could hear them whispering, mostly in English, but every now and then she caught some Spanish words and felt small doses of relief.

She looked again at the big boy. He paced around the batter's box, swinging down in harsh jerks at the air in front of him. With each hack at nothing, his arms seemed to swell even more, making him bigger and bigger. When he noticed her looking at him, he spat on the dirt between them.

Startled, Fernanda turned back to the huddle. The boy who had been pitching, his eyes shaded under the brim of a turquoise hat with the same A as Ernesto's, was talking to her. He asked, in Spanish, how long she had been watching them play. She hesitated. It had been at least two weeks, but she always ran and hid if a ball was hit near her. She looked away and shrugged her shoulders.

"Man, what's the deal? She don't speak Spanish neither? I thought you said she was Mexican, Nesto," the boy who had been playing shortstop said.

"Chill, Quen. She speaks Spanish and some English, too. She's just shy, you know?" Ernesto turned to her. "*¿Verdad?*"

Fernanda nodded.

"*Bueno,*" the pitcher said. "Ernesto says y'all are family, so I'll go ahead and introduce you to everybody. *Yo soy* Gabriel. That big boy," he said, pointing to the player at home plate, "is Gerardo, and that's Quen" he pointed to the boy who'd asked if she spoke Spanish. "You already met him." Then he pointed at a tall blond boy who had been at first base. That's Robbie."

Robbie nodded.

Gabriel turned to Fernanda and asked, "*Pues,* what do you wanna do?"

III.

"Hell no, she ain't using my glove," Gerardo sputtered, still holding the bat like he was ready to use it.

"Come on, G," Gabriel pleaded, "don't be like that, man. We can play with a full outfield this way."

Gerardo did not budge. Fernanda could see his grip tightening on the bat. Without looking at her, he said, "Man, look at her tiny ass hands . . . She won't be able to do shit with my glove on, anyway."

Gabriel sighed, turned towards the others and shrugged.

Ernesto stepped in. "Robbie, you mind playing with G's glove?"

Up to this point, Robbie hadn't said a word. Maintaining his muteness, he shrugged his shoulders and nodded. In-sync, he and Ernesto tossed each other their gloves. Robbie put on Gerardo's glove and started pounding his right fist into it.

"You mess up my glove, I'ma beat the shit outta you, Robbie," Gerardo said, pointing at him with the bat.

Robbie smirked, flipped off Gerardo with his throwing hand and jogged back to first. Ernesto then put on Robbie's glove and gave his own to Fernanda. They turned and jogged towards center and right field. Gabriel went back to pitching, and Quen moved to shallow left field.

Gerardo stayed at bat. "You guys finally ready?" he shouted.

Everyone crouched, smacked their fists into their gloves. Fernanda tried to mimic them. She bent over, tried to let her hips sway naturally, but she could feel her blood pulsing just beneath her skin and her knees trembled.

Gabriel went into his windup and delivered. Gerardo swung hard. He missed, and the ball smacked against the wooden backstop.

A chorus of "ohhhh" came from everyone out in the field.

"*Pinche* Gabriel," Gerardo yelled, pointing at the pitcher with his bat. "Don't be tryin' to get all cute just 'cause there's a girl watchin'. I know you ain't got more than two pitches, fool."

Fernanda snuck looks at everyone, just to see if this comment were something they were all thinking. None of them seemed to react, though. They all got back into their crouches.

Fernanda could feel sweat stinging her eyes, but didn't dare look away from the batter.

Gabriel wound up and delivered another pitch.

Gerardo swung hard again and nicked the ball, sending it rocketing off the top of the backstop and onto the grass behind it.

"0 and 2," Robbie yelled from first base and threw his hands in the air to give the announcement a monumental feel.

Quen and Ernesto both yelled unintelligible things, like creatures in the night communicating across distance. Then they hushed, and Gabriel went back into his windup. He delivered again. Gerardo swung.

Then came a sound like the sky breaking open, and everyone began to shout as Ernesto raced towards the fence at the deepest part of center field.

Fernanda didn't move. Even though she was in right field, she could hear Ernesto panting, forcing himself against the wind to stop the ball from hitting the ground. He took flight and stretched his arm as far as he could. Boy, ball and ground collided with soundless impact. No one moved. Ernesto lay on his stomach, waving his glove over his head like a flag.

Fernanda realized she hadn't taken a breath since Gerardo hit the ball. She suddenly inhaled so hard it caused her to cough. The sound brought all movement back. In an instant, Ernesto was on his feet, jogging casually towards them, flicking the ball up and catching it in his ungloved hand. Shouts and cheers welcomed his slow trot back to position. Right as it looked like Ernesto was returning the ball to the infield, however, he instead turned and tossed it to Fernanda.

"*Allí te va*, Fernanda," he said and zipped it to her as though it were guided by a laser.

With no time to think, Fernanda closed her eyes, raised her left arm and opened her gloved hand as wide as she could. A half-second later, a thud accompanied a small and exciting pain in her palm. Relieved, she examined the worn-down ball inside her glove. She let the fingers on her right hand tickle the rust-colored stitching, as though it were a precious stone.

Shouting from the infield brought her back to reality. She had another test before her. Fernanda had practiced for this moment by watching baseball games and mimicking the throwing motions. In Obregón, she would walk home from school, throwing rocks deep into alleyways as she went. With those memories playing in her head, she stepped forward, let her arm swing around her body and released the ball towards the infield.

Gabriel, who seemed surprised by Fernanda's power, had to stretch his arm over his head and take a step back, but the ball found him. He laughed and yelled, "One down, two to go!"

Quen, Robbie and Ernesto all smacked their throwing hands against their gloves and yelled at different times, "Two to go!"

Without enough people for teams, each person would get to bat until they were out three times—either by strikeout, pop out or a 5-3, 6-3, 4-3, 1-3 ground out. Nobody played catcher because no one had a catcher's mitt or equipment. For most of the game, Gabriel pitched, but others also stepped in at times.

As the afternoon light eased towards dusk, it was Fernanda's turn to bat. She picked up one of the two bats resting against the backstop. Its weight surprised her, and she could not hide the effort it took for her to swing it, feeling her entire body pulled by the bat's momentum. She put it down, picked up the other bat. It was even heavier. Her confidence began to crumble, and she thought about telling the others she just wouldn't bat, but what would they say? Weeks of work trying to find something, anything to call her own and everything was about to be lost because she could not swing the heavy bat well enough to hit a pitched ball. No, she wouldn't quit, she told herself, not after getting this far.

Fernanda flexed her arm muscles and picked up the first bat again. She rested it on her right shoulder and walked to home plate. From home, she looked up at the pitcher's mound and her chest tightened.

Standing there, a smile stretched across his wide face, was Gerardo.

He raised his hands as he spun to look at the fielders. "*Todos están listos* for El Rey to show y'all some nasty heat?"

Quen and Gabriel jeered, but the others just waited for him to pitch. Fernanda could barely look at him. In the early evening light, he looked as big and impenetrable as a wall.

"What about you, *nena*? You ready?" he said over his glove.

For Fernanda, throwing was something she had practiced, even if it was mostly with rocks, and catching was all about trusting her hands. But how a swinging bat synced with an incoming fastball was still a mystery to her. She had only swung pipes and sticks at rocks she had lobbed to herself, and her success rate there was minimal. She tried to conjure images and memories she had seen of baseball games on TVs in stores and restaurants back home, but all of it suddenly felt foggy and unreadable. She thought about her grip, her legs bending like she had seen the boys do, her eyes focused on the ball in the pitcher's hand. Gerardo went into his windup.

What else did batters do? Then a booming thump made her mind go blank. Gerardo's fastball whooshed right past her and banged into the wooden backstop. She jumped back, away from the speeding ball.

"Strike one," Gerardo shouted and put his finger up in the air.

Fernanda, trying not to let the bat slide off her shoulder, walked over and picked the ball up. Her attempt to throw it back to the pitcher only made it about three-quarters of the way before rolling to the edge of the mound.

"Really?!" Gerardo said, theatrical in his movements and sighing as he went to the ball and picked it up.

"Man, hurry your slow ass up," Quen yelled from between third and second. "It's gettin' dark."

Gerardo ignored him and went back into his stance. Fernanda stepped back into the batter's box. This time she mentally went through everything and focused on the movements of the pitcher. He wound up and delivered. She swung and missed. The same loud thump marked the ball's destination.

Again, she walked to the ball, picked it up and heaved it awkwardly back towards the mound. Walking back to the plate, she noticed Ernesto in shallow center miming a batting stance. His elbows tucked, feet spread, knees bent, torso rotating with an exaggerated swing. Fernanda nodded, just a little, and stepped to the plate. She tried as best she could to re-create what she had just been shown. This time she tried to time her reaction.

Gerardo wound up and pitched. Fernanda swung, and felt a surprising thwack ring from her hands. The ball whizzed over first base, and the first-baseman charged after it. She watched it for a second before remembering to run. She dropped the bat and tried to coordinate her arms and legs, but stopped, when Robbie lifted his arms and yelled, "Foul ball!" still chasing the travelling baseball.

At a loss, Fernanda walked back to home plate and the batter's box. As she got back in her stance, she noticed that Gerardo was looking down at the ground. She wondered what he might be looking at, but suddenly he wound up, pitched and before she could think of anything else, she felt a punch in the middle of her back.

All that Fernanda could do was let out a yelp as she fell to the ground and clutched at the dirt. Her vision came back slowly, blurred by tears. She could hear everyone yelling. In the dying light, she could barely distinguish the bodies on the mound. She reached a hand back to where she felt the burning ache, but she couldn't touch it. As she felt all her emotions flooding over her, she looked one last time at the group of screaming shadows on the pitcher's mound. One began to jog towards her, but she didn't give it a second thought. She got to her feet and ran towards the park's exit. She ran like everything and everyone was chasing her, trying to trap her, trying to keep her from getting away. She cried like she had wanted to ever since she'd arrived in this awful place. This place her mother had lied to get into, this place where she was always stupid or shy or quiet. Where she was never welcomed and where she did not want to stay.

Fernanda came to the street she lived on. She ran past Ernesto's house. How could she ever face him again?

Inside the sorry-excuse-for-a-house, Fernanda buried her face in a pillow on the old mattress. She howled all she could into the cushion. Her shame, she told herself, was her new home. She could never go back.

IV.

"*No empieces*, Fernanda. It's been a long day already," Flor said.

"*Por favor, mamá*. Can we please go back home?" Fernanda pleaded.

This was the new ritual. Fernanda would spend the day at school trying not to draw any attention to herself. Then she'd race home and sit on her bed until her mother arrived in the evening—exhausted, dragging herself from the front door to their tiny bathroom for a shower and then to the bed. Flor usually went to sleep as soon as her body went down. But when her mother emerged from the shower before getting into bed, Fernanda would take the opportunity once again to try to convince her. Later in the night, she would wake up to make them both food for the next day, but it was usually too late for Fernanda to stay up.

"*Ándale, mamá,*" Fernanda said. "How long are we going to be like this?"

Sitting on their bed as she dried her hair, Flor would lose her patience. "*¡Ay, Fernanda, por favor!* Just go do your homework or go play *béisbol en el parque* with your *amiguitos.*" She'd wave at Fernanda as though she were a fly.

One evening, mid-ritual, there was an unexpected knock at their door. They froze and then heard another more forceful knock.

Flor's eyes were wide, and she began to tremble. Could this be the visit they were warned about? The inevitable punishment for Mexicans who dared to lie and trespass? It felt like all the oxygen had left the room, Fernanda heard a familiar voice. "Hola, Fernanda, you home?"

Relief came over her and she ran to the door, opening it to see that Ernesto was turning away, about to leave. He wore a grey T-shirt and blue jeans. His purple hat had its brim pushed up on his head, revealing his short black hair matted down on his forehead with sweat.

He smiled as soon as he saw Fernanda. "*¿Qué onda?* Long time," he said.

Fernanda was silent at first, but after avoiding him and the others for weeks, there was something about Ernesto in the evening light that made her feel better.

"*Sí,*" she said, finally. "How are you?"

Ernesto laughed. "Aww man, *mero-mero, pero aquí* tryin' to stay alive, feel me?"

Despite having improved her English, Fernanda had no idea what Ernesto had just said. "*¿Qué?*"

Before he could answer, Flor came to the door.

"*¿Cómo estás, m'ijo?*" she said

Ernesto immediately straightened up and said, in his cleanest Spanish, "*Buenas noches, Señora. Estoy muy bien, gracias. ¿Y usted?*" He even went so far as to tip his hat, like a true *caballero.*

Flor let him in and they made small talk. Fernanda stayed at the door, looking out into the neighborhood and recalling how scared she had been when she first heard the knocking.

Suddenly Ernesto turned and, patting Fernanda on the shoulder, said, "So, what do you think? You comin'?"

Embarrassed over having missed the first part of his request, Fernanda shrugged and turned to her mother.

"*Bueno*, Fernanda," Flor said. "If you would like to go to Doña Carmen's house to watch the baseball game between the Dodgers and the Diamondbacks with your friends, you can. Just make sure you are home before it's too late out."

Fernanda felt a sparkling in the center of her stomach. She turned to Ernesto. He was smiling. She nodded her head. The Dodgers against the Diamondbacks! she thought.

Back in Obregón, people all over the city supported the Dodgers. Restaurants and bodegas played their games on TV. And the older folks talked constantly about Fernando Valenzuela, the famous *indio* pitcher from Etchohuaquila, Sonora, as though he were still playing. Posters and photos of him were all over town. A *tío* had even once told Fernanda that she had been named after him. Whether or not it was true, this story had made her pay extra attention to anything about the Dodgers.

Inside Ernesto's house, Don Mario and Ernesto's *tío* Pepe were already sitting in front of the TV when Fernanda and Ernesto arrived. They greeted one another, and she was overcome with excitement but also homesickness. The sound of grown men arguing about which baseball player was capable of what reminded her of what she had left behind in Obregón. She wondered whether she would ever see home again.

Just when she was sinking back into her loneliness, however, Gabriel, Gerardo, Quen and Robbie walked in.

"Oh, damn, look who's here! ¿*Cómo estás?*" Gabriel reached out to greet Fernanda like they were family.

The others all turned to Gerardo and made jokes about his pitching. They said he needed glasses, that he was scared to pitch straight up to Fernanda because he was afraid "she'd knock one out of the park." Fernanda did not understand the phrase but felt okay smiling.

As they laughed and got louder, Don Mario yelled at them to settle down. "*¡Ya!* If you kids wanna *chismear*, go outside. We're here to watch the *pinche* game," he said.

"Mario!" Doña Carmen cried from the kitchen. "Watch your language around *la niña*, please. *¡No seas tan bruto!*"

This shut everybody up.

The game began at last. Fernanda watched every pitch in awe, barely hearing anything said by the older men or the boys. Then, in the second inning, with no runners on and no outs, a batter for the Dodgers hit a homerun, and Fernanda lost control. She screamed in happiness and clapped a lightning beat. As the batter triumphantly ran the bases, Fernanda felt as though the team were welcoming her to this country. Her celebration was cut off when Ernesto tapped her shoulder from behind.

"What are you doing?" he said, looking confused.

Fernanda then noticed that no one else was joining her, the way people in Obregón would have. She pointed at the screen. "The Dodgers scored a homerun, they're winning."

"*Híjole*," Ernesto's *tío* Pepe said. "Don't tell me we got Dodgers fans living in our backyard." He laughed and elbowed Don Mario in the ribs, but Ernesto's dad barely smiled. The boys all stayed quiet.

"What did I do wrong?" Fernanda said.

"Oh, it ain't no big deal, really," Ernesto explained. "But, like, the D-backs are our home team. They're from Arizona, so we cheer for them."

Fernanda nodded, trying to take in this news. She had never considered how much closer this sport was for people on this side of the border.

Ernesto seemed to understand Fernanda's confusion, and so he kept explaining. "So you probably think the Dodgers are, like, a team of Mexicans, but the D-backs got *mexicanos* playin' for them, like their pitcher, Armando Reynoso, he's from San Luis Potosí. He's the one who just gave up that homerun. And they got another *mexicano*, Erubiel Durazo, he's from Sonora, like our *familia*. I think he was born in Hermosillo."

"The D-backs are ours," Gabriel piped in, "our team in Arizona."

"Yeah, we get to be the first ones ever to cheer for 'em," Quen said. "We didn't get 'em from some other city or other fans who didn't want 'em."

"They belong only to Arizona," Ernesto said. "Kinda like all of us, you know?"

Fernanda nodded again. She belonged.

"Plus," Gerardo said suddenly, "fuck the Dodgers."

The boys and men all laughed at this.

Fernanda's head rattled with all this new information. As the two teams traded hits and strikeouts, the Diamondback rallied in the bottom of the ninth inning but still lost by a score of five to four. She wasn't sure how to feel. It seemed like her past had finally caught up to meet her here in this new place, wrapping itself around her body and keeping her close to what was familiar. And yet she suddenly wasn't sure that was what she wanted. Despite the hometown team's loss, Fernanda felt a warmth in the room that she hadn't known before.

After the game was over, as Ernesto accompanied her back home, she wished she could hold onto that night the way she held onto memories of Obregón.

V.

Lucky for Fernanda, the next day after school she got a chance to relive the night. Rather than hurry home, she met up with Ernesto and they walked back to the neighborhood together. Along the way, they met up with Gabriel, Quen and Gerardo. The boys competed to tell Fernanda all about their hometown Major League team. Two years ago, the D-backs had started out struggling, but they had surprisingly had made it to the playoffs. Last year, they finished third in their own division and didn't make playoffs at all.

"Back in '99, we should've even made the World Series," Gabriel said.

"Yeah," Quen said, "the damn Mets got lucky against us, but then they got their asses whooped by the Yankees."

"But, like, don't everyone get their asses whooped by the Yankees?" Gabriel said and laughed.

"But not us," Ernesto said. "Trust me, *esos hijos de la chingada* ain't trying to see us in the World Series. Especially not this year. Think about it." He started counting off his fingers. "We got Johnson, Schilling, Gonzo, Durazo . . . "

"Wooo!" Quen said and pretended he had just touched something really hot with his hand. "Talk that talk, homie!" He shoved Ernesto playfully.

They all laughed with pride, including Fernanda.

"Aw, shit, y'all are really trying too hard just 'cause there's a girl here, huh?" Gerardo said and snorted.

The energy dried up like spit on hot pavement. Fernanda looked at the boys, but none would look back at her, their heads down or facing away. They walked like that for a few horribly quiet moments, until Ernesto put his arm around Fernanda and said, "Don't even listen to G. He's just still mad because of how well you did against him during your first at-bat." He smiled and patted Fernanda's back. She smiled, too.

When they arrived at the baseball field, Robbie was waiting near a dugout, next to a shopping cart containing the boys' gloves, their two bats and a few baseballs. Everyone seemed to lighten up because it was time to play. This time, Fernanda knew exactly what to do.

She fielded several positions as they took turns batting. She chased down grounders, caught pop-ups and relayed throws from everywhere, moving from right to center to left to third to short and then to second. Finally, it was her turn to bat. This time, Ernesto pitched to her. As she warmed up, swinging the bat at home plate, their eyes met. They smiled and exchanged nods.

He delivered his first pitch. She swung hard and sent the ball high into the air.

* * *

That night, the Diamondbacks played against the Colorado Rockies. Everyone gathered at Ernesto's house again. Fernanda got to see the pitcher named Randy Johnson, a tall, angry-looking man with a *bigote* and long, brown, curly hair flying out the back of his cap. He reminded Fernanda of the older men in Obregón who rode around on motorcycles with their dirty, long hair dancing like fire from underneath their helmets. Randy Johnson struck out fourteen batters, throwing every pitch, it seemed, as hard as he could but somehow never being satisfied with how hard he was throwing.

The Diamondbacks won the game 7 to 3, thanks not only to the fierce pitcher but also to a homerun hit by the outfielder Luis Gonzalez, who Fernanda thought was *mexicano* but was actually the son of Cubanos. The boys had all jumped excitedly when he hit his homerun in the first inning.

"That's what I'm talkin' about, Gonzo!" Quen shouted.

"He's got nine long balls already this season, man," Robbie said. "He's gonna hit so many more. Man, this team!"

Fernanda felt the same excitement and warmth she'd felt from the previous night, but this time she felt less fearful that it wouldn't last.

VI.

Soon it was late May and the school year had ended. The Diamondbacks had won ten games in a row to become the leaders in their division. Fernanda no longer thought about leaving El Valle. She had done well enough in school to pass on to the seventh grade, and she was even looking forward to possibly sharing some classes next year with Gabriel or Ernesto or Quen, or even Gerardo.

Throughout the summer, they played ball during the day, in scorching heat and white sunlight. At night, they gathered to watch the Diamondbacks. Although she kept her Dodgers hat, she thought of the Diamondbacks as *her* team. Depending on where she played in the field, she tried to imagine herself as one of the players, tried to imitate their movements, their spirits.

At bat, she alternated stances depending on her mood. When she was energized, she stood and swung like the speedy Tony Womack. If she was methodical and trying to calculate where best to place a single, she was Steve Finley. On rare occasions, when she felt herself powerful and ready to shatter the world, she was a blend of Durazo and Gonzalez—taking large swings and either missing everything or putting it all into the booming crack of her bat. She could only dream of hitting an actual homerun, but she told herself if she was given enough time and practice, she would eventually get a ball across the fence, never to return.

At home, Fernanda told her mother all about her latest feat on the field, and Flor, in turn, talked about some of the people who worked with her at the hotel where she cleaned rooms.

"*Están locas.*" Flor joked. "They're all so crazy but very kind and open. And you're never going to guess what they keep telling me, *m'ija.*"

"What's that, *amá?*"

"*Bueno*, these women say the government of the United States is talking about extending amnesty to many *mexicanos* who currently live and work in the country but don't have papers."

Fernanda could feel her pulse in her ears. She was speechless.

"I still don't think I believe them. I'm not sure where we would fit in all these plans," Flor continued. "But if it happens, it could maybe mean we relax *un poco, pero también*, it would mean we could visit Obregón without worrying about how to come back to El Valle."

VII.

It was a Tuesday morning. Fernanda had been in the seventh grade for about a month. She woke up, ate the *huevos con papas* left for her in foil in the kitchen and read a note: "*¡Feliz día, mi hermosa!* I will see you tonight with your cake! :)"

Fernanda smiled so big and kicked her feet against the legs of her chair. She quickly finished eating, washed her face, got dressed and went to Ernesto's house so they could walk to school together.

While they walked, they talked excitedly about the Diamondbacks playing the Rockies that evening. They were both confident they would win because Johnson was pitching again, but one never knew with how unpredictable baseball could be, especially as teams prepared for the playoffs.

After a moment, Fernanda could no longer hold in what she was thinking. "Ernesto?"

"What's up?"

"Do you know what today is?"

"Uh. The eleventh?"

"Uhmm. But do you know what else it is?"

"No, What?"

"It's my birthday," she said, looking down.

Ernesto stopped, and Fernanda left him a few paces behind. "Hey! *¡Feliz cumpleaños!*" he said, ran up to her and put his warm palms on her shoulders. "How old are you now?"

Fernanda picked her head up. "I'm twelve," she said and smiled. "*Nací en* 1989."

"*Órale.* You and me got fall birthdays. Mine's coming up in November, but I was born in 1988."

This made her smile. She was spending her first birthday outside of Obregón. She usually never talked to her new friends about anything except baseball and some things about México but she was excited. To her it was right that Ernesto was a little older. He seemed wiser. He was the one who knew the most about what she had gone through since crossing the border in March. Lost in her thoughts, she realized Ernesto was talking to her.

"Wait. What did you say?" she said.

He laughed. "Man, where do you float off to when you do that?" he said and pointed out towards the horizon.

Fernanda felt her face get hot; she looked back at the ground.

"Aw, c'mon," Ernesto said. "If I can't be messing with you on your birthday, then how do I know we're for real *familia*?"

Fernanda couldn't hold in her laugh. She looked back up at him. "All right. What were you saying?"

"*Eso es,*" he said. "What do you feel like doing to celebrate your birthday?"

Fernanda thought for a moment and shrugged. Then she told him what she normally did on her birthdays. "My *amá*, usually bakes me a cake, and sings 'Las mañanitas' because it's always been just the two of us."

"*Pues,*" Ernesto said, "you're here with all of us now, so we should all try to do something together, you know? Like, maybe we can go to a baseball game or something."

Fernanda's body filled with electricity. "Really?"

Ernesto nodded. "For sure. It might be too late to get tickets for tonight, but I bet we could try to get my dad and my *tío* to take us. They've been trying to go see a game for a while. Plus, it's your *cumple*, so it'll be, like, special, you know?"

Fernanda didn't know what to say. She wanted to hug Ernesto and for them to be able to go to the game right then and there. She wanted to sing and to scream and to cry and to tell her mom and to be by herself so no one would see her do all these things.

* * *

When they arrived at the school yard, they noticed that kids were huddled in packs, talking in low voices. As Fernanda and Ernesto walked past them, the kids looked at them up and down and then went back to talking in their circles. When Ernesto and Fernanda found Gabriel, Gerardo and Quen, they were standing around a basketball hoop lazily throwing a basketball up at the rim. Nobody knew what was going on.

Once the bell rang and all the kids walked slowly into their classrooms, Fernanda found out what was wrong. In her first period Language Arts class, the teacher told them that the country had been attacked. They did not know who attacked them, but the attackers had used planes to blow up buildings and kill people in New York City and other places. Fernanda felt stiff, like she knew more bad news was coming. The kids were told to read quietly for the rest of the period.

Later that morning, Fernanda's American History class gathered their things and walked down the hall to another classroom. Once there, she saw another group of students seated at their desks, their heads all turned toward a corner of the room that had a television playing and replaying footage of a plane flying into one building, while another building on the right sprayed smoke like blood from a wound. Fernanda turned away from the television. She saw Ernesto at the front of the room. He looked lost, too, and this scared her almost as much as what was on the television. When he saw Fernanda, though, his features lifted a bit and he gave her a "*¿Qué onda?*" nod. Fernanda nodded back. When she tried to go to where he was sitting, however, her teacher told her to return to the back the of the room where her classmates all stood. She remained there until they were allowed to sit on the floor. Then the teachers tried to answer questions from students about what they were watching and what they might need to do next. By lunchtime, the students were marched to the cafeteria and allowed to eat. After that, everyone was told they could go home early.

On the walk home, neither Fernanda nor any of the boys said anything. They barely looked anywhere but at the ground or directly ahead of them. When she and Ernesto got to his house, they went in and turned on the TV in the living to try to take their minds off what they had seen. Still, neither of them spoke.

Fernanda felt like her head was under water. After a few hours, they turned to a local news station and found out that all baseball games had been cancelled and would be postponed for a week while everyone in the country tried to figure out what to do next. Water swirled around Fernanda's head.

VIII.

Never again did Fernanda and Ernesto talk about attending a game. Fernanda's mother, it turned out, did not have enough time to buy cake ingredients the day of her birthday. She and Flor had to postpone their usual tradition until the following Sunday, when they had a small get together at Ernesto's house with all the family, the boys from the neighborhood and some of their parents, as well.

While the adults talked in the kitchen, the kids sat in the living room and tried to piece together what they knew.

"This shit is crazy," Quen said.

"Word," said Gabriel. "How the fuck do people even do this kinda shit?"

"My folks say it's 'cause they don't do enough to check who the hell's coming into our country, you know?" Robbie said. "And at my school, teachers are saying we gotta stop letting people in at all, 'til we know what's going on."

No one said anything. They all looked in different directions. Finally, Fernanda, who had grown to hate the quiet and the way it always crashed into her life to ruin things, spoke up. "What the hell are you talking about, *cabrón*?" she said while she smacked the armrest of the couch.

Robbie's eyes got as big as the room, and everyone held their breaths. Then Gerardo's snorting laughter broke it.

"Holy shit!" Gerardo screamed nearly loud enough for the adults to hear and clutched his stomach. He could barely breathe. "Yo! I didn't know the girl had that kinda fire in her." He wheezed. "Robbie, you best watch yourself or this Mexican girl's gonna kick your ass."

Fernanda felt oddly comforted by Gerardo's barking laughter. Something about his venom being directed at another target for once made her feel like she had done something right. Before anyone could say anything more, Ernesto's *tío* Pepe burst through the front door, breathing hard, with hardly any color in his face. He went straight to where the adults were huddled.

Ernesto and Fernanda knew something else was wrong. While the others went back to talking about Robbie and baseball and the playoffs, Fernanda and Ernesto watched, soundlessly, as Pepe relayed some awful news to the other adults. Flor looked at Ernesto's *tío* and then it looked like she was staring out into nothing. Don Mario went to put his arm around his brother, and Doña Carmen did the same for Flor. All four of them then realized they were being watched by their children, but didn't hide their pain. Fernanda and Ernesto were speechless, wondering what more had been lost.

* * *

A few days later, Fernanda and Flor sat in their one room house. They waited for Don Mario to bring them food. Neither of them spoke. Fernanda had stopped wondering how long she would live in this kind of quiet. Her life was only quiet. Having her mother near did little to comfort her at this time. This, more than anything, weighed on them: the knowledge that mother could no longer do anything for daughter, nor daughter for mother. They shared helplessness.

The night of Fernanda's party, Josué, the man who had helped them cross the border, had been caught trying to cross into the United States with more people using more fake documents. Ernesto's *tío* Pepe—who sometimes worked with Josué on different things—said it was likely Josué would try to reduce his punishment by giving the names and as much information as he could about other people he had helped cross. Flor was afraid to return to work and afraid to let her daughter return to school. They became prisoners in an enormous jail cell. Their only contacts became Don Mario and Doña Carmen and Ernesto, but even these three tried not to visit too much during the day, lest they draw some observer's attention.

Days passed. Nothing happened.

Ernesto was the most consistent visitor. He came in the evenings, bringing food his family had made for their dinner. He and Fernanda sat on the back porch of his house and talked about school. Although he wasn't in the same classes as Fernanda, Ernesto tried to bring her updates on her homework. At school he told the teachers she was very sick and couldn't come to classes or that she was caring for a sick relative or that she was visiting family out of town.

"I'm not sure how many of them believe me, but who cares. If they want, they can call our house and my mom will tell them one of those things," he said.

"Yeah," Fernanda said. "But it's not really a lie. I feel like I *am* sick or caring for someone else who is . . . "

"What do you mean?"

"*No sé*," she said. "But it's like Robbie was saying, about the country needing to check who comes in. It feels like we're sick people who have to be kept out or in small spaces where we don't see or talk to anyone else. It makes me feel like I shouldn't be here."

Ernesto didn't say anything. In the dimming light, they could hear crickets chirping and the distant sounds of cars on the road. As Fernanda felt the familiar dizziness of her head under water, Ernesto scooted right up beside her and put his arm around her shoulder.

"I know you're not sick," he said. "And you *should* be here. You belong here, with all of us, and we're not going to let anyone keep you anywhere," he said. The imaginary water tank that trapped her head shattered, and for once Fernanda felt it was okay to let things be silent.

IX.

Eventually, Flor went back to work. They needed money. This was an unavoidable truth about this country. No matter how afraid they might be, they needed money, needed to be part of everything happening or else they would die. The same was true for Fernanda and school. So they tried to go back to how they were. Fernanda's grades had suffered, but most of her teachers liked her, and she worked hard to make up some work. Unfortunately, this meant she no longer had time to play baseball with her friends in the evenings.

Ernesto told her it was all right. "The baseball postseason's starting," he said. "Everybody just wants to go watch those games instead of playing, anyways."

This comforted her. As she worked day and night to catch up and feel once again part of this world, she also sensed people around her becoming consumed by other things. She noticed more flags and banners—for the Diamondbacks and for the United States. For Fernanda it felt like everyone wanted to show off where they lived, but she did not know what that meant for somebody not born here. Did Americanos really know what their country meant, or could they ever imagine what kind of place it was for people like Fernanda and Flor? Fernanda knew answers to these questions would not be easy, but she also felt she could find them out one day.

In the meantime, the Arizona Diamondbacks had made it to the World Series to play the New York Yankees. More than usual, Fernanda thought about the attacks in September. For the people of New York, she thought, seeing their team win must feel so important. She knew the Yankees were a very good team that did a lot of winning, and this meant that others did not like them. At least, that was what she had learned from her friends. She tried, with no success, to ask Ernesto about what it meant that the Diamondbacks were playing the team from the city that had been attacked.

All he said was, "New York experienced something really terrible, but this is about baseball and our chance to win something as Arizona. We have to try our hardest."

She did not bring it up again. It had to be something only Americanos understood.

The week of the final series, they gathered at Ernesto's house to watch every minute of every game, even the ones that lasted until one in the morning. Every game had its own mixture of magic and tragedy. Games 1 and 2 were both exciting. Everyone sat entranced as Arizona's two best pitchers helped secure relatively simple victories. Games 3, 4 and 5, however, were jittery heartaches. No matter how well Arizona played or how hard they competed to take a lead into the final inning, it seemed like every night ended with the young Diamondbacks' closer Byung Hyun Kim in tears. Sleepy and drained, the kids dragged themselves around for a few days, nervous at the idea that their team was one loss away from ultimate defeat.

But Fernanda felt at peace. She did not think the loss would be so bad. She told herself it was inevitable.

In Game 6, they watched Randy Johnson and his angry throwing return to dominate New York. The Diamondbacks scored fifteen runs and won easily. Still, Fernanda would not let herself believe.

Then came Game 7. It was a cloudy Sunday night in November. Fernanda watched with everyone else as the Diamondbacks and the Yankees kept each other scoreless for much of the game. Then, in the sixth inning, the Diamondbacks scored, and Ernesto's house burst with cheers and claps.

"*Eso es todo,*" Don Mario said definitively.

One inning later, though, the Yankees scored, too, and then they scored again the very next inning. After the Diamondbacks did not score in the bottom of the eighth, Fernanda felt like, somehow, she was responsible for this. She knew she could not win, and neither could those around her. So, while Randy Johnson went out to pitch against the Yankees in the top of the ninth, Fernanda looked at the pained and anxious faces in the room. Johnson got out of the inning without allowing another run. To Fernanda it didn't matter. She knew the Yankees had an amazing closing pitcher. She sat back on the couch without being noticed and tried to capture everyone in the room, just an image in her mind of how they were, for her own safekeeping.

The bottom of the last inning, however, started with Mark Grace singling to centerfield, and again everyone cheered. Next,

Damian Miller bunted, but rather than throw the pinch runner David Dellucci out at second, the Yankees pitcher threw the ball to centerfield in an error. The cheers inflated into roars. Even after the next batter's bunt was fielded and used to throw out the lead runner at third base, Ernesto and everyone else still clapped.

"We got this," he said. "We got this!"

Fernanda sat up and looked at Ernesto. His eyes were fixed on the next batter, his hands clutched around his neck, his Diamondbacks hat pushed so far up his head it was a wonder it hadn't fallen off. He really believes it, she thought, he really believes he deserves to be part of something good, to be a winner. Suddenly, she heard a crack ring out from the TV and Ernesto jumped up in the air. Tony Womack had hit a double to tie the score. The boys jumped around and high-fived one another. They sat down only when the next batter came to the plate.

It was Luis Gonzalez. The bases were loaded. The score was tied at 2-2.

"C'mon, Gonzo," Gabriel said with his hands together like he was praying

"Let's go, baby, let's go," Quen kept saying over and over, his arms wrapped tightly around his torso.

"*Vámonos*, Gonzo," Gerardo said.

Fernanda had never seen him like this, his hands fidgeting from his mouth to his neck to his thighs and back together. He had rubbed parts of his face so much, they glowed maroon against his brown skin.

The first pitch was delivered and Gonzalez fouled it back. Everyone rose and fell like a chest taking in a hard breath, trying to stay alive.

Fernanda didn't know why, but she tapped Ernesto on the shoulder. Without missing a beat, he turned to her. His eyes were wide, his jaw clenched, almost like he was scared, but he tried to relax it a little, for her. Fernanda could then feel her pulse quickening, it beat in a tempo she had never known before. It was not the fastest her heart had ever beat, but it was different, a stranger kind of anxiety. She leaned forward, close to Ernesto's face, and said, "*Gracias*, for letting me be here, at home with all of you."

As Ernesto's face eased into smile, a thwack came from the TV, followed by a collective chaotic howl. They had won.

Boxhood

"Man, I ain't bullshittin'." Paolo smacked the counter, held eye contact with the cashier.

The lone Circle K employee looked unconvinced. But he couldn't keep his focus on the boy in front of him because of the other three boys roaming the shelves of candy and chips. Thanks to Alan, Dolfo and Martín, Paolo knew he had the higher ground in this face-off. He held steady, refusing to pay more than the refill price for the fresh cup of soda he'd just poured himself.

The cashier surrendered. "All right, but don't be coming in here trying to pull this shit again," he said and rang up Paolo. "Don't think I won't call the cops on you punk-ass kids."

Suddenly, he looked up. "Hey!" he shouted at Dolfo and Alan as they walked towards the door. "Don't you two leave before I can check your pockets."

No sooner did the cashier yell than Dolfo was off like a bullet, leaving Alan, frozen, alone.

"Get over here, kid," the cashier ordered, motioning with his index finger.

Alan, feeling his heart beating hard, tried to read Paolo's face for anything that could help, but found his older brother was looking past him.

"Yo, what the hell happened over there?" Paolo said and pointed to something behind Alan.

Expecting to see a tidal wave or some other punishment coming to crush him and his cousins, Alan turned slowly. Outside, the blue sky had dark gray spilled all over it. Clouds almost never showed up in the summertime in Arizona. The smoke was so out of place against the normally empty sky, it hung there, as if it would soon start raining in the middle of a 100-degree-plus day.

Everyone stared in silence.

In fact, only one person wasn't distracted and that was Martín. He snuck up behind Alan and hissed, "Run, fool!" Both kids bolted. The cashier said nothing.

Paolo hesitated for a second before grabbing his soda and racing out the door after them, towards the source of the smoke.

* * *

Two blocks away, Paolo arrived at the smoldering remains of a house. Firefighters stood idle, talking among themselves, and Paolo remembered in second grade when the teacher asked the class to draw a picture of what they wanted to be when they grew up. He drew himself in a red coat and red hat, holding a snake-green hose that spat blue and purple at a brown house. His remembering was interrupted when he noticed one firefighter staring at him and his crew. He shook the picture from his mind and, catching his breath after running, he stood straight up to meet the firefighter's gaze. He put his chest out and tilted his head back like *cholos* used to do and looked down his nose at the firefighter: *¿Qué pues, güey?* Whachu lookin' at? The firefighter stared at Paolo for a moment. Then, like nothing, he turned to talk to another firefighter.

"Dumbass junkies burned their house down," Dolfo said and bit into a stolen candy bar. He laughed with a mouthful of chocolate and nougat.

Noticing how few people had been drawn to the smoke, Paolo got an idea. "Let's go into the alley and see if we can sneak into the backyard."

Martín and Dolfo nodded. Alan didn't nod but didn't have a choice either way. Paolo scanned the house once more. Its history did not matter to him; what mattered was what this random fire might bring. He and his crew headed to the end of the block and turned onto Booker T. Washington Street.

They were about to reach the alley, when Martín whistled. They all looked up to see an El Valle PD cruiser coming.

They froze.

In the driver window, behind sunglasses, a cop scanned them up and down as he drove by. It was anyone's guess what he was doing in the hood: responding to the 9-1-1 fire call, cutting through on his beat or looking for kids like Paolo and his crew to harass on an otherwise boring summer's day.

"You kids stayin' outta trouble, right?" the cop said. His face was hard, the words were a threat, not a question.

Still puffed up from staring down the firefighter, Paolo wanted to show the cop he wasn't afraid of any words or uniform, but Dolfo and Martín spoke up quickly, using their white voices.

"Yes sir, officer!"

"We will, sir!"

Martín even saluted like a soldier to a commanding officer in the army. The cop turned his head and his squad car roared to the end of the street.

"Man, fuck five-O," Dolfo said, back to his normal voice.

"Hey! What if he heard you?" Alan said in a hushed yelp. He was three years younger than Dolfo and Martín, four years younger than Paolo, and still young enough to feel scared about having stolen from a store.

"That fool can't do shit to us," Paolo scolded his brother. "Come on, let's go."

At the alley, they moved into their positions: Martín walked to the corner and took off his shoes and hid them in a neighbor's bushes. Almost everywhere in the hood there was a pair of sneakers hanging from a telephone wire, so pretending you were trying to get "your" shoes down always worked to buy time. Dolfo and Paolo bent down to re-lace their sneakers tight, and they brought their shorts up to their waists and secured their belts to make sure they wouldn't drag. Dolfo looked up and down Washington one last time. They were ready to go.

"Wait!"

They stopped with a jolt and turned.

"What, Alan?" Dolfo said, rubbing sweat from his eyes with his shirt.

Alan was new to hanging out with the older kids. Normally he was at home watching TV or reading a book or doing anything else where he wasn't in the way.

"I ain't fast like you guys. . . . What if the cop comes back or someone sees us?" Alan asked.

Paolo swelled with the anger and unleashed it in a smack upside Alan's head. "Quit being a little bitch!" he said.

Without a sound, Alan clutched where his brother had hit him as if pieces of him could fall off and smash against the ground. Head low, he walked into the alley.

* * *

Behind the house, intermixed smells of shit and burnt, rotting wood assaulted their senses.

Paolo pulled his collar over his nose, but it didn't help much. He, Dolfo and Alan stood there, staring at the house and trying not to get sick. He wanted to leave, but he couldn't. He'd come for something, anything, and he wouldn't leave with nothing.

Suddenly they heard a whistle in the distance that meant Martín had seen a cop or someone else who could get them into trouble.

"Man, there ain't shit here except the smell of rotten ass." Dolfo spat. "Let's bounce."

Paolo turned toward where they had entered the alley and saw Martín run by, with both shoes on, purposely not looking towards them. Time was up.

They turned to walk back down the alley.

Abruptly, Alan spoke up. "Hey. What's that over there?" he said, pointing towards the house. Paolo and Dolfo followed Alan's line of sight to a medium-sized box up against the house, surrounded by dirty rags, rusted tools and singed weeds.

Paolo wanted it. He gave his cousin a knowing look. Dolfo glanced down the alley towards Washington and breathed deeply—he was the fastest of his cousins, maybe the fastest person in the hood; in his twelve years of life, he'd outrun more cars, cops, bullies and sorry-excuses-for-stepdads than anyone could count. He was up and over the chain-link fence in a move so smooth that any comic book superhero would've wanted to see it again to take notes.

Dolfo crept towards where the box sat, spitting and gagging all the way. As he knelt to pick it up, like something straight out of a horror movie, the house's back door crashed open. In the doorway, looking like the type of faceless phantoms the boys saw in their nightmares, was a firefighter with an axe in his hand, his face in a mask.

"Hey!" he wheezed, "what the hell are you kids doing?"

Dolfo snatched the box and ran to the fence. He hurled the box over and then flung himself over too. In an instant, he was nothing but kicked-up dirt and a memory.

Paolo grabbed Alan by the shoulders and yelled, "Run!" after Dolfo had tossed the box over the fence. Alan went flying down the alley, in the opposite direction of Dolfo. As the oldest and biggest, Paolo knew it was on him to secure their score. He bent down and picked it up. It was a little heavy, but he was able to handle it. He looked up and saw that the firefighter had taken off his mask and was looking at him with pity or disappointment or maybe jealousy.

"*¡Chinga tu madre, cabrón!*" Paolo yelled and took off, following the same path he'd sent his scared brother down. He ran hard, struggling with the box all along the way.

* * *

"*¡A la chingada!*" Martín sounded like he was going to explode. He, Paolo, and Alan were at their hideout behind their *tío's* house. "We hit the jackpot, fool!"

The box they had taken was filled, from corner to corner, top to bottom, wrapped in protective plastic, with porn magazines. Martín didn't know what to do with his hands or his eyes: all the blood rushing at the same time to his chest, his brain and his barely pubescent dick.

It was as if they'd been stranded on a desert island, and this box was their first contact with the world beyond, an unexpected relief package. Who knew what else could wash up on their shores? Paolo wondered about these possibilities, but he couldn't focus on them, because he couldn't stop thinking that he hadn't seen Dolfo since the alley, a half hour earlier. What if he'd run into trouble?

"Hey, so, did you see where Dolfo ended up running to?" Paolo asked his cousin.

Martín did not even look up. He was so absorbed in the box's contents. Of all the cousins, he was the craziest about girls and their parts. When he was seven, he had found some magazines in his dad's closet, and when his dad caught him looking at them, the ass-whooping he got let him know that this stuff was especially off limits. Since then, he wanted to see and know more.

Paolo got tense. "Hey, *pendejo*," he said and reached out and swatted a magazine out of Martín's hands. "I said, 'Did you see where Dolfo went?'"

Martín snapped out of his trance. "Uh. Yeah," he said. "Last I saw he was running towards the projects. He probably went to his house or to lay low with Quen or Sergio." He shrugged. "It ain't like anyone could catch him, anyway."

Paolo relaxed a little and picked up a magazine. The women on the cover were all wearing big sunglasses, some had their hair dyed orange and some green, and they all had on shiny, silvery outfits as if they had traveled back from the future just to be in a porn magazine. They reminded Paolo of some of the stories he liked to read, the ones about people exploring new planets and trying to determine if the aliens they met were friendly, deadly or both.

He looked over at Alan and saw he was staring at the box. His eyes grew, trying to take in all the images. Paolo realized that all of this was new to him, including the hideout behind Tío Salo's house. His mother wanted him to spend more time with his brother, though. She'd scolded Paolo for not including his brother in what he did and she scolded Alan for being inside all day by himself, "*como un enfermo*."

"You know you're not saying shit to Ma about this, right?" Paolo said.

Alan looked at his brother, more confused than scared. "Y-yeah."

"Word," Paolo said. "Now, quit staring and get in some of this shit, it won't hurt you." He laughed.

* * *

After dinner that night, Paolo was washing dishes when Alan came into the kitchen.

"Lolo," Alan said, "do you think it's okay that we left that box behind Tío Salo's house?"

"I told you, you gotta quit bein' a *nena*, man," Paolo said without turning from the sink.

Alan got quiet. Over the sound of the water, he heard the TV in the living room and knew his mother had fallen asleep on the couch again.

Paolo kept washing, kept his head down. "Nobody ever goes back there, so there ain't nothing to worry about. Plus, Tío Salo works nights and he ain't even awake during the day, you know?"

He turned to put a cup on the rack and didn't realize Alan was right behind him. The cup hit Alan in the face, fell and shattered against the tile floor.

"*Pues, ¡¿qué chingados hacen?!*" The words thundered from the living room.

"Yo, get outta here!" Paolo said just above his breath and shoved his brother.

Alan stumbled out of the kitchen like a cockroach given a second chance.

Shortly after, their mother came into the kitchen. Paolo was kneeling, using one hand to sweep the glass shards into another. He didn't dare look up, even after he saw her feet right below his nose. He knew better than to stand in any position that could be seen as challenging, and cowering wouldn't do any good either. So he knelt and waited.

The hitting started. He could hear the hard thuds as much as he could feel them against the back of his head. His vision went black and when it came back, he saw the floor and the glass and his hands through tears he could not control.

His mother's voice boomed. "*¡¿Qué pues, cabrón?!* I wake up too early! I work too hard for you to be *tan pendejo!*"

Paolo did not make a sound, did not lift his head. He thought, briefly, about standing up, just this once, and fighting her, but instead he kept sweeping and trying to force the tears back to where they belonged. Maybe he would finally do something, but first he would pick up every piece of broken glass, no matter how small.

Suddenly, silence. After a few moments, he felt her hand. It rested on the back of his head, fingers running through his hair. He stood up and saw her crying. He couldn't do anything more. He was taller than she was—had been for years. She leaned in and hugged him, and he hugged her, still holding broken glass in one hand.

* * *

Although it was more shaded than anywhere else in the alley, the lot behind their *tío's* house was not spared the triple-digit summer heat.

It was Alan who, after flipping through a couple of pages in a magazine, broke the silence and said, "Are we really just gonna hang out here all afternoon?"

"What's the problem, man?" Dolfo said and put down the *Play Like a Girl* magazine in which naked women were pictured playing sports.

Paolo noticed the magazine and remembered a spread where all the women were completely naked except for scarves, hats and ice skates. He imagined himself naked on the ice with them: all of them chasing after one another for warmth and fun. He wiped at his face angrily and snapped. "Yeah, Alan, the hell's your problem?"

"It's just really hot." Alan shrugged and looked at his feet. "I don't have a problem."

Visions of smiling girls, free nakedness and cooler weather: they were all just ideas and distractions. Sweat, heat and dirt, that was real. His brother's whining was also real.

Dolfo turned to Paolo and said, "I mean, maybe we could try to go get a soda or some shit from the Circle K?"

"Oh, okay then. You got money?" Paolo shot back.

"I mean . . . nah," Dolfo recanted.

"And what about you, fool? 'Oh, it's so hot,'" he said to his brother and mimed wiping tears from his face. "'And I can't keep myself from sweatin' like a little bitch.'"

Alan felt his face get hotter. Being family, for him, was a test he couldn't stop failing.

"That's what I thought," Paolo said, but he wasn't done. "Unless you wanna try to steal some more shit, especially when they'll be lookin' extra hard at us right now, then guess what?" He looked to his cousin and then to his little brother. "We ain't doin' sh . . . "

"Hey!" a deep voice called.

Paolo froze. His hands mid-gesture, panic screamed inside his body.

A second later, Martín appeared from behind a wall, laughing his ass off. He made his voice deep and unrecognizable again. "What're you little wetbacks doing back here? Playing with your *pingas* or what?"

Dolfo joined and even Alan found himself laughing a little with relief.

Paolo could not laugh with them. He was still heated. "The fuck's your problem, fool?"

"Chill, chill," Martín said, finally coming down from laughter. "Chill. I was just messin' around, man." He brought his palms to his chest to try to catch his breath.

"Damn, Lolo," Dolfo said wiping tears from his eyes, "you shoulda seen your face when you thought Tino was five-O." Paolo relaxed to barely smile at Martín. This time, Martín had gotten him and gotten him good. "So where the hell you been, man?"

Martín reached into his pocket and pulled out four crumpled dollar bills. "Yo, so check this shit out. You know Mikey? He saw me with a magazine and gave me five bucks for it. It was a pretty shitty one, too; like, one where the girls barely show anything. Horny little fool probably ran all the way home with a boner." He laughed.

No one joined him in laughter this time.

Instead, Dolfo wiped the sweat from his face with his sleeve, stood up and walked towards him. "Hey, so, we each get a dollar then, right? You said you got five?"

Martín stopped laughing in a flash. He shut his fist and shook his head. "Uh-uh. It was my idea. If you want money, go sell some yourself, man."

Dolfo stepped to him. "You ain't keepin' all that money, fool."

Paolo rushed to put himself between the two, his back to Dolfo. "All right. Chill. Chill."

Martín, suddenly brave behind his human shield, held up the money and said, "You want money, Dolfo? Go ask one of your daddies for some."

He'd lit the fuse.

Dolfo didn't know who his dad was, and his mother wouldn't or couldn't tell him. Dolfo didn't have a dad, as far as he was concerned, and anyone who said otherwise was bound to catch the hell he carried inside him.

"I'm gonna fuck you up, motherfucker!" Dolfo said.

Paolo felt Dolfo push him into his back and felt his hand near his ear. Paolo turned around without thinking and shoved Dolfo to the ground.

"Back up off me, asshole," Paolo yelled. Dolfo hit the dirt but was up in a flash and was about to retaliate, but Alan stepped in between the two of them. He didn't say anything, but he looked like he was getting ready to start screaming and never, ever stop.

Paolo felt the heat hanging on him again, felt like he was boiling in dust. His anger was for Dolfo, then for Martín and then for the box. He looked to where it sat and considered its blame in this.

"Lolo!" Alan screamed in a high-pitch voice.

Paolo shook out of his thoughts. He took a few deep breaths, turned to Dolfo and gave a half-frown, not an apology, because apologies didn't mean anything between boys. He let him know that it wasn't time for them to try to break each other. Then, he turned to Martín, standing with the money in his fist at his side. "You ain't keepin' all that money," Paolo said. "Dolfo, Alan and me almost got caught tryin' to get that damn box. Or . . . ," he said and shrugged, " . . . you keep what you got so far, but you can't have any more. It's your choice: *familia* or money, man."

Martín hesitated for a second, but then gave them each their dollar. They were, for the moment, family again. "For life, *ése.*" Martín smiled.

He and Dolfo and Paolo and Alan all dapped each other up and laughed.

"That's what I'm talkin' about," Dolfo said, almost singing. "Yo, now we can hit up the Circle K, Alan." He patted Alan on the chest.

Alan nodded and smiled.

"Word," Martín said. "Y'all already know I'm tryin' to get me a big-ass cold pop."

As they left, Paolo put the box in its hiding place between two cinder blocks. He covered it with the dirty plastic tarp they'd found in an alley.

* * *

The rest of the summer crept by like the sun across the Arizona sky, forgettable but not without consequence. They met daily in the park or at someone's house and went over to the vacant lot behind their *tío's* house. The abandoned car frames and overgrown weeds worked as cover. They were careful not to be followed. This protected their business. They'd sell a few torn-out pages at a time for whatever sum a kid could afford, and they'd always find a way to divide it among themselves, even a token amount to Alan, who never sold anything.

After school started, the four walked together in the mornings while the temperature was climbing to its usual three-digit high. Alan would peel off at Polk Elementary School and the other three would keep walking the last few blocks to Roosevelt Middle School.

One morning, Dolfo asked Alan, "Hey, so what you think about tryin' to sell some of these at Polk, man?"

Paolo and Martín shifted their glances from Dolfo to Alan. No one said anything. When Alan finally did talk, it wasn't what Paolo expected.

"Do you have any with you right now?" Alan answered.

Dolfo looked at Paolo for the final word. Paolo nodded, and Dolfo reached into his backpack and took out two magazines. Alan took them without a flinch and put them in his Ninja Turtles backpack—once Paolo's.

"*Órale*, Alan!" Martín said and clapped. "You're growing a pair of *huevos, ése!*" He pounded his palm against Alan's chest.

Alan tried to laugh. He looked at Paolo, who smiled and quickly hid it.

"Yo. Let's go. I ain't tryin' to be late to school again," Paolo said. "The teachers at Roosevelt are already looking for any excuse to hate my ass."

They walked at a quicker pace the rest of the way.

* * *

"Paul?"

Paolo picked up his head to see Mrs. Pruitt standing right in front of his desk with her arms crossed.

"Would you like to share your latest 'masterpiece' with the class, or would you rather put it away and get back to reading?"

The class buzzed like mosquitos around his ears.

Paolo clutched the piece of paper with the rocket ships and space weapons he had drawn, then crumpled it up in one hand.

"I finished my book already," he said as his head sunk below his shoulders. On the first day of class, he had found *The Illustrated Man* in the library. He read it in no time, and he wanted to create his own stories that he could draw and tell to strangers he might meet out in the middle of nowhere.

Mrs. Pruitt did not budge. "Well, school's been in session long enough for you to know what to do, right?"

Paolo said nothing. The mosquitoes were inside his head; he felt his skin get hot all over.

Mrs. Pruitt sighed and said, "Well, class will be over in ten minutes, so there's no sense in sending you to the library now. Make sure you come tomorrow with a new book to read during reading time, okay?"

He didn't move or talk, afraid that he was one big mosquito bite about to burst.

* * *

"Man, fuck Mrs. Pruitt!" Paolo said to Martín and Dolfo as they walked to their hiding place after school. Alan hadn't met them outside of Polk, but they figured that he'd probably gone straight home after school.

Martín laughed. "Aww *pobrecito*. Is that *vieja* being mean to you? That's what you get for testing into Advanced English, fool."

"She's just a bitch." Paolo spat, ignoring the last bit about his testing placement.

Dolfo joined in, laughing. "*No llores pues*, poor baby."

"Man, fuck you two," Paolo said as they turned the corner near their *tío's* place, but before he could say something else, he felt like he was being watched. He stopped and turned around and saw Victor a few feet behind them.

Paolo and Victor had been in the same classes from kindergarten to fifth grade, but Victor hadn't made it past there. Even though he was thirteen, he was still at Polk, and he was big for his age. At Polk, he looked like he should be hanging out with the teachers, not the kids. Paolo didn't know what he was up to, but he knew it couldn't be good.

Victor walked up to them and put a cigarette in his mouth, smiling a serpent smile.

"Wassup?" he hissed through the cigarette.

The three of them remained quiet, trying to hide their fear that Victor was so closed to their hiding spot. Could he know?

"Yo, Paolo," Victor said, "so, this where your little pervert brother found the shit he had at school?"

Paolo stiffened.

Victor chuckled. "How bad is your ma gonna whoop him, huh? I know Mexican ladies get crazy when they're mad, yelling all that *chinga chinga chinga* shit!" his voice went high.

No one said anything.

Victor lit a cigarette and took a drag. "So should I tell the teachers and kids at Polk to start planning a funeral, or what?" He blew smoke into Paolo's face.

"You're bullshittin', man," Dolfo said, trying to cover for his cousin.

Victor kept smiling. "Swear to god," he said and crossed himself, "he got caught with some magazines at recess. I guess he was selling them or some shit. What a little fucker!"

Coldness stabbed through Paolo.

"Yup," Victor said and blew out another stream of smoke. "They suspended his ass and everything. Y'all should reel him in. Who knows what other crazy shit he'll get into next?"

Victor's brown skin and hair made him look like he could have been related to them. His mom was Pima and Maricopa. But Victor had been born and raised in the barrio where they lived and not on the rez. Even though no one had ever seen his dad, some people said he was Mexican, too. But Victor didn't speak Spanish and didn't want to. He always told people he was "half-Indian, half-fuck you."

"So, y'all gonna show me the rest, or do I gotta get an adult involved?" Victor warned through a cloud of smoke.

Paolo swelled with adrenaline. He took off like a jet. He barely felt his arms and legs pumping, could barely hear Martín and Dolfo call Victor a *puto* and a *pendejo* behind him. Dizzy, his ears full of wind and heat, he sprinted all the way home.

By the time he got to his house, covered in sweat and out of breath, he had almost convinced himself Victor had just been messing with him, and Alan would be watching TV or reading a book in the living room. As he burst through the side door, though, into the kitchen, he heard the TV, and his heart sank. His mother had left work early—everything was worse than he thought. He tried to slow down his breathing before going into the living room to face her.

"Don't even try, *cabrón*," she said without looking at him. Still in her work uniform, her hair was up in a bun the way they made her wear it at the restaurant. Through gritted teeth she said, "I work all day. I do everything for you *chamacos*. I don't deserve this." Her voiced cracked.

This was a limit Paolo had never known. He didn't know what would happen next.

Without turning from the TV, she lowered her voice and growled, "*Lárgate*. Get out. I have to work a shift tonight to make up for cutting my morning short."

Paolo left in silence.

In Alan's room, he found his little brother lying in bed under the covers with his back to the door. Paolo walked over to where Alan was and put a hand on his shoulder. The small body underneath the covers trembled. Alan was crying, but barely making any noise.

* * *

"Hey, so, your brother didn't tell anybody except Victor about the box, right?" Martín asked a few days later as they walked home from school.

Paolo ignored the question.

Martín tried to talk through the silence. "I mean, 'cause, you know, we talked with Victor and we might still be able to sell stuff at Polk through him."

Paolo picked up his pace and walked ahead of his cousins.

After that, they stopped walking to school together. Instead Paolo went to Polk early in the morning to drop off Alan's homework from the previous day and pick up the homework he had to do that night. Then, after school, Paolo walked home by himself to get Alan his homework right away. The two of them would hang out at home together doing chores, doing homework and doing nothing until their mom arrived. This, Paolo thought, was his way of making Alan's suspension go by faster.

Sometimes, on the walk home, he saw Dolfo and Martín walking with Victor a few blocks ahead of him. He didn't try to talk to them or stop them. At school, he overheard kids talking about the three of them: how they hung around the elementary school selling things. Thinking about this made Paolo walk home faster, hoping to speed time up. Soon, he told himself, things would be like before.

* * *

When Alan's two-week suspension ended, he and his brother walked to school together. Alan finally revealed to Paolo how he had been discovered. Victor had heard he was selling magazines and made him tell where he found them or he would snitch to a teacher. Scared, Alan told Victor, and Victor told other boys to try to get more kids interested in buying. When word spread to a teacher, Alan tried to get Victor to help him hide the magazines, but Victor played dumb. Alan got suspended.

"But I never snitched on you guys, you know?" Alan said, looking up at his brother as they walked. "I didn't wanna do that to family."

Paolo forced a laugh because he didn't know what else to do. He couldn't imagine his brother holding strong while teachers grilled him about getting suspended and called his mom to come get him.

When they were near Polk, Alan said, "So, do you think we can chill with Dolfo and Martín after school today? I know they couldn't come by the house while I was suspended, but I wanna hang out with them again."

"For sure," Paolo said without thinking and nodded.

Once he was walking on his own to Roosevelt, he tried not thinking about Victor. He told himself, since Alan's suspension was done, they'd go back to the way things were; be boys, be family.

On the walk home from school that day, though, any idea of going back to their old ways disappeared like smoke into the sky. When they turned toward their *tío's* street, they saw two cop cars with lights flashing in front of his house. They saw their *tío*, looking tired and terrified, talking to an officer at his front door. On the trunk of one of the squad cars, they saw the box sealed with yellow police tape. Paolo felt his stomach churn as he took a few more steps and saw three heads in the back of one squad car. He didn't need to see their faces to know who they were, to know what this was. He turned to Alan, put his hand on his shoulder. They walked home in silence.

* * *

"*Pero ¿cómo es posible?*" They heard their mother say into the phone. "How is this possible?"

Paolo and Alan ate their dinner and listened to her talk with Dolfo's mom.

"For how long? *Ay Dios*. I'm telling you, these kids and this neighborhood—nothing good comes from it."

"So," Alan whispered, "do you think Dolfo and Martín will be okay?"

"I don't know, Alan," Paolo said without looking up from his plate.

"Well, do you think they'll say anything about us?" Alan asked.

Paolo finished his food but kept his eyes down and said nothing this time. When he was done, he got up to go wash his plate at the sink. Over his shoulder he said, "There ain't anything they *can* say. We weren't there."

They heard their mother's "bye." Then the approaching footsteps. Paolo kept his back turned. Alan sat still. They both waited to see what kind of mood their mother would be in.

"Did you get enough to eat?" she said, her voice like a breeze through a desert, when she entered the kitchen.

"Sí, Ma, it was really good. Are you going to sit and eat, too?" Alan said.

Paolo kept his face turned away, his head down, eyes closed, afraid to believe.

"No, *mi'ijito*," she said. Paolo could feel her sad smile on his back. "I think I'm going to go lie down for a little bit."

Alan let out an "Mmm-hmm," and kept eating.

"*Gracias, m'ijo* for washing the dishes," she said..

Paolo nodded at the sink and barely got out a "*De nada*, Ma."

He heard the kitchen door swing closed, and he turned on the water. Warm, it ran over the back of his hand and dripped onto his plate. When he was sure she was in her room, and he could no longer stand there, Paolo turned off the faucet and went to the living room. When Alan was done, he got up, washed his plate and finished washing his brother's plate, too.

Mari's Shot, Reshot

Abuelo died before I was born, so I never got to know him—at least, not the living version. His ghost appeared to me in high school, though, and as I get ready to graduate today, I wish he'd leave me alone. Can you believe he's still holding a grudge because I quit wrestling?

"*¡Pinche chamaca floja!*" he says, shaking his ghostly fists at me as I get dressed for the commencement ceremony later this evening.

Thankfully, I never learned much Spanish, so I just pop in my headphones and keep getting ready. Eventually he gets tired and goes quiet.

* * *

It started my freshman year at Desertwood High.

It sucked. A lot. Especially for a girl like me. I got my ma's thick, Mexican hips and my dad's white freckled, bony shoulders. The other girls in their one-color cliques never left me alone. Gym class was by far the worst of it. As we ran laps, girls would say all kinds of horrible things.

"Pick up the pace, *Cinco de Mayonnaise*."

"Let's go, *white-back*."

"Outta the way, you halfie bitch."

The last girl shoved me and I fell into some mud next to the track. Laughter from the other girls assaulted me like car alarms.

Suddenly, from somewhere, cutting through all the noise, I heard a voice say "*¡friégatela, m'ija!*" right into my ear.

I got up in a flash, even with my bad Spanish I know what that meant, and did just that. I charged at the girl, drove my shoulder into her stomach and took her ass down. As she scrambled beneath me, I went to work. I tried to choke and twist and pull until something snapped. I felt a rush of strength I had never known before. A far-off battle cry roared inside me, a warrior's heartbeat. It was Abuelo.

After I served my week-long suspension for fighting, I was again in gym class. I was supposed to be running laps but Coach Martínez pulled me aside.

"What are you . . . ?" he said.

But just as I felt the same familiar bite of that question, he quickly followed up. " . . . 'bout 112? 115?"

"What?" I said, because neither of those were slurs I'd heard before for being mixed-race.

"Your weight," Coach said. "Listen, you got a solid base and shoulders made for pain." He squatted, smacked his thighs and arms. "Plus, that kind of aggression you displayed the other day is perfect fuel on the wrestling team."

He said "team" like a secret only insiders knew. I wondered if he'd also somehow been alone in high school. Had a dead ancestor also helped him channel loneliness and anger into strength?

I hesitated for a second. I didn't know a single thing about wrestling except for the goofy *lucha libre* stuff some of my younger cousins watched sometimes. I wanted to tell Coach I didn't think this kind of thing was for me, but then I heard— again like it was far away and also within me—a voice say, "*¡Vamos muchacha!*"

"I'm in," I said.

With Abuelo in my ear and in my heart, I drilled and trained like a girl possessed. During matches, just like when I fought that girl on the track, Abuelo's chants and cheers filled me with a force I couldn't explain, but I knew what to do with it.

Then school didn't suck so much. I'd spend mornings running and doing some push-ups and pull-ups with Abuelo cheering me on. I'd come back home, shower and bike to school. Before the bell, I'd meet up with some of the guys from the team and we'd talk about our upcoming matches and what we were gonna eat after we were done cutting weight. At lunch, we'd sit together and joke about who had to face-off against a beast this week and what we could do together and individually that year at state. Later, at practice, we'd beat on each other until we became a team. By my senior year, I was co-captain and had earned the distinction of All-Region 106-pounder. I even placed third at the state tournament, and we took bronze as a team.

We celebrated afterward. Coach grilled *carne asada* for the team, and I could hear Abuelo laughing and cheering as though he was also celebrating our trophy.

Best of all, I finished high school. Wrestling got me through it. I was even a little sad for it to end . . . but only a little. Mostly, I was glad to be done with it all and to move on. But Abuelo didn't get it. He didn't understand why I rejected a Division III scholarship offer from somewhere in Idaho to stay and attend the local university with my friends instead. Abuelo wasn't having it, and he let me know.

For the remainder of my senior year, Abuelo never left me alone. While I watched TV, he would change the channel to boxing. When I wanted to sleep-in on weekends, he would try to wake me at ungodly hours to go run or jump rope. I told him the season was over, I was done with all that, but he didn't want to hear me. He was so extra. Eventually, I started sleeping with earplugs in my ears and a crucifix and dreamcatcher by my door to keep him out.

* * *

"Ma," I say as she finishes my make-up and fixes my hair under my graduation cap.

"What is it, Maribel?"

"Was Abuelo, like, a good athlete when he was alive?"

"Not really, *m'ija*," she says. "He was pretty short and never very fit. I remember him being pretty uncoordinated and clumsy, too."

"Really?"

I look in the mirror. Abuelo is messing with my reflection, fattening my face and neck. I blink hard and he's gone.

"Well, was he, like, a big sports fan?"

Ma snorts. "Only if you think training roosters and betting on them for cockfights makes you a sports fan."

Roach Meets the Surf

The Greyhound drummed through the desert. All around her, Roach saw nothing but dirt and cacti and dirt and rocks and dirt and no clouds and dirt. Nothing felt different, except for her. As she watched everything glide by her window, the sun filtered through the tinted glass and made her drowsy. She felt herself drifting and she let her mind wander to what was behind her.

* * *

Roach first noticed the letters when she was seventeen. Holding the envelopes against the light, she could see they had checks inside of them. By her senior year of high school, Roach was ditching regularly to come home and watch TV or read whatever she could in the newspapers about the latest crime discovered in the Arizona desert. It was during these ditch rituals that she figured out that the checks typically arrived monthly, on or around the fifteenth. By the Spring, she waited for the mailman and for the opportunity to look, in peace, at the address from which the checks came. They were from California, and they were for a few thousand dollars each.

One time, the summer after she barely graduated with her diploma, she decided to try to cash one of them herself. She took the envelope to the check-cashing place a few blocks from her house, but as she stood in line, she realized she didn't have any way to prove she was her mom. Even if the place went ahead and did it for her, she still had to go home and answer for the missing mail. Besides, what would she do with her sudden surplus of cash? For that matter, what were the odds that the clerks would keep their cool after seeing a teenager cashing a check for a few grand? These roadblocks were enough to scare her off. She needed another plan.

"Hey, Babe," Roach said to her boyfriend Troy while he watched professional wrestling on TV one night. "What would you do if you never needed to work for money?"

"Ya mean, what if I'd grown up like some spoiled-ass, rich kid?"

"No. . . . Like, what would you do if you could do anything you wanted? Like, if there were some things you didn't have to worry about, and you could be whatever."

Troy turned up the volume on the TV. The only voices in the room, then, were the announcers talking about an upcoming grudge match.

"Uh-na," Troy mustered after a while.

Roach alternated between looking at him and the TV. After a few moments of trying to figure out why an overweight shaman in a leopard skin loincloth was fighting a spandex-clad man with a mullet, or why Troy seemed completely entranced by this scuffle, she decided to go study in his bedroom.

Later, Roach lay in bed next to Troy. The heat from sex dissipated from their bodies faster than usual as Troy began to snore. Listening to him drone on and to the cars rumbling on the nearby freeway, Roach tried to imagine a future where she and Troy had no money worries. It was beyond her imagination. If she didn't have to worry about money, wouldn't she have her own car? Wouldn't she have her own place? Wouldn't she leave El Valle behind like explosions in the action movies she and Troy liked so much? If I had a lot of money, would I keep any of this? she asked herself.

What could her mom possibly be doing with the checks she received every month? She worked hard, Roach knew; she probably worked too hard, if anything. Plus, her mom was always complaining about how thankless and miserable her job at the hospital was. As Troy's snoring intensified, Roach wondered how much pretending her mom was up to just to keep the money a secret. It was one hell of an act, she thought, and, as Troy drowned out all the other night sounds, she got angry imagining herself as the unknowing rube to some big charade. Only a sociopath or straight-up bitch would keep this act up. And only a dumbass, sorry bitch would do nothing about it, she said to herself.

To calm herself a little—and to try to ignore Troy sawing wood—she counted all the clues she'd collected. The checks arrived just about every month. They came from an address in Santa Monica, California, but no name on the return address. *Who could be sending the money?*

If only her mom would tell her, Roach might even consider letting slide that she'd ever kept the secret in the first place. At dinner one night, Roach remembered, she tried to hint to her mom that she was willing to let bygones be bygones, if she'd only consider relocating them to better surroundings.

"I think we would be better off if we, like, could move to the east side, to a nicer part of the Valley . . . or maybe out of Arizona completely. Like, I've heard people say Southern California is really pretty and super safe."

"Is that right?" her mother responded as she took a forkful of noodles to her mouth.

Roach had made spaghetti and meatballs as a peace offering.

"So, tell me," her mom said, "would living near a beach have kept you from quitting softball or math club? Would it have kept you from hanging out with those punks with spiky hair? Would a beach make you do better than a 2.2 GPA and barely getting a diploma?"

Roach said nothing. Her mom kept going.

"I already *sent* you to school on the nicer side of the city, and *still* you managed to throw away your chances at success, Roxana." Roach's mom was the only person who still called her by her given name. "Your problem, dear, is that you always try to find the easiest excuse not to do something. You always look to blame your environment rather than learn to work harder for what you want."

"Oh yeah, 'cause if I just gave it 'the ol' college try,' I might someday be able to dream of being a single-mom and nurse who owns a crappy two-bedroom, right?" Roach fired back.

She had crossed a line, as she often did in these arguments.

As usual, her mom went silent.

This silence was the same silence Roach met if ever she mentioned the absence of her dad. It was impossible for her to ignore a father-sized hole in her life when most of her friends had them, and Father's Day came around every year to reinforce their importance. When Roach was younger, she asked about her dad, but her mom didn't budge. She shook her head and told Roach not to think about that because it wasn't worth thinking about. They were fine, she'd say, and she'd move on.

Things changed when Roach became a teenager. One day in third-period gym, Roach was up at bat during a softball game. When she stepped to the plate, she heard a girl say something about how Roach better get good at handling poles because that's all girls without dads were good for. Roach took the first pitch, a called strike. At the next pitch, she swung hard and hurled the bat towards the dugout where the girl sat—her screams were satisfying to Roach, and she had to keep from smiling outside the vice principal's office while waiting for her mom to come get her.

On the drive home, her mom complained about having to leave work early. The vice principal had threatened to involve the police if she didn't come for her immediately. From there followed a flurry of questions Roach grew accustomed to hearing as she got older. What were you thinking? Why do you act this way? Don't you realize how stupid that was? Do you have anything to say?

She only ever had one response. "Why the hell did you even have me if you couldn't keep my dad around?"

What had begun with her curiosity became a weapon. Roach brought up the topic of her father only to cut at her mom during arguments.

* * *

The next morning, in her Intro to Film Studies class, Roach tried to find the right words for how to break up with Troy. She decided to embark on a trip to trace the money back to its source, and she needed to tie up all her loose ends. Professor Fred was talking about the twilight of the studio-model for Hollywood in the 1970s. Terms like *termination, dissolving, independence* and *freedom* invaded Roach's already-cluttered brain, but she tried to fight through it. She had to push forward, against the lecture and the boredom of the class and of herself. She finally gave up on thinking about the wording as Professor Fred's lecture touched on Martin Scorsese's *Mean Streets* and its characters' inabilities to escape the violence of their circumstance.

Instead, she weighed the pros and cons of having sex with Troy one last time.

Pro: it'll probably help calm him down and make the whole thing just a little smoother.

Con: he might try to coax her into something extra, like butt stuff, or some other fetish he'd been hiding.

Pro: she might be able to burn away all the nervous energy she'd been collecting since she finally decided she was going to leave.

Con: Troy maybe wasn't perfect, but he also wasn't horrible. He didn't deserve this. No one did, really.

A few days later, Roach did the deed. She posed as her mom to cash the most recent check with a sketchy clerk at one of those places people without bank accounts used. With that, she had locked herself into running away. And her new life she'd pursue alone, with no traces of her old self. Anyone or anything that might stand in the way had to be handled and forgotten.

Later that evening, she broke up with Troy. She reassured him that, "Yeah, I know you're not really crying, you're just emotional. Yeah, it makes sense. Yeah, I'll for sure remember all the good times we had. Promise." They shared one last, long kiss but did not have sex. Troy, it turned out, was never in it for that.

The following morning, instead of catching the 104 bus to El Valle Community College, Roach ducked into a Circle K and waited, with a cup of coffee and two powdered donuts, for her mom to leave their house. In her backpack, she had the cash from the check, but she needed more time to pack other things she would need, since she didn't really know how much time she would be spending on the road. As soon as she was sure her mom had left for work, she went back to her house and packed whatever she could fit into a duffle bag. She left a note that read:

In case you don't notice, I left. Don't waste your time looking. You can't "afford" to take the time off work anyway, right? Troy might be by to cry to you because he's got nowhere else to go. He doesn't know anything except that I left EV.

-R

Ps. If I see HIM, you probably won't hear from me again. Enjoy the rest of your life. It's been real.

* * *

The bus rattled, then jolted, to a stop. Roach woke up, immediately alert. Excitement bubbled in her stomach. This was it! She looked out her window and saw only a small trailer sitting at the edge of an otherwise deserted parking lot. This was it?

Around her, a few passengers gathered their bags and made their way down the aisle towards the exit, while a few others remained seated, some still sleeping. Roach, again, looked out her window and tried to figure out why Los Angeles looked like nothing more than cracked asphalt and a set of railroad tracks that seemed as though they hadn't seen any use in decades.

"'Scuse me," Roach said to one of the passengers getting off the bus. "Do you know if we're going to any other stops in LA? Or is this it? Or . . . " She trailed off when the man, wearing a thick gray hoodie despite the April heat, looked at her like she was the dumbest person alive. They stared at one another, stuck in the awkward moment.

"You ain't been to Cali before, huh, girl?" he said. He smiled despite missing many of the necessary teeth to pull it off.

She felt her face get hot and her chest tighten. Shit. A few hours out of El Valle and already she was showing herself to be totally lost. She had to show she was in control.

"Well . . . " Roach stretched her arms and yawned, trying to play off her confusion as sleepiness. " . . . I just was sleepin' the whole time, so I'm kinda out of it, you know? Just wanna make sure I don't miss my stop 'cause my whole family's waitin' for me. Mom and dad got huge plans, so they definitely don't want me to miss my stop, you know?" She punctuated her performance with a smile.

The guy's face crumpled, his lips tightened. Roach worried this stranger was offended by her crappy lying skills. As he went to say something, the driver turned and shouted at them.

"Hey, Craig, you gettin' off, or what, man? Irma's gon' be waitin'."

Craig snorted. He sized Roach up one last time and exited the bus. She watched him leave, walk across the parking lot and disappear out of sight. I don't see anyone waiting for him, she thought.

"This is Blythe, Miss," the driver said. Roach met his eyes in the rearview mirror. "We'll be in LA in about two and a half hours, and your family can pick you up downtown."

Roach nodded at him. She sat back in her seat and leaned her head against the window, closed her eyes and exhaled. She didn't know who or what was waiting. She knew only that somewhere in Santa Monica was the source of the money in her backpack. She needed to find it.

* * *

Downtown LA also offered no signs of the beach or movie stars. It was maybe ten or fifteen degrees cooler than it had been in El Valle, but that felt like the only real difference between the two. Otherwise, so many things were the same: same cracked sidewalks, same barely-held-together rattling of old cars, same kinds of people pushing shopping carts full of junk. Same Roach.

After a moment, she shook her head and started walking away from the bus station. She had no idea which way was anything, but she knew that she needed to get to Santa Monica, and she also guessed she was nowhere near it at the moment. She walked. And she walked. As she walked, the buses, cars and homeless people made it impossible for her not to think of home. The more downtown LA did its impression of downtown El Valle, the more she thought that maybe, just maybe, changing herself would be much harder than she originally planned. Then a flash of panic—maybe this wouldn't be an ultimate escape. Maybe she'd soon find herself, like when she was younger, again in front of her pissed-off mom, trying to explain this mess.

I'd rather try to work something out with those homeless folks, she thought and kept walking. For hours, she walked. She stopped only in the familiar confines of a 7-11 to get a soda and some chips for dinner. Once she reasoned she was far enough away from the bus station—too far to turn back before nightfall—she reached into her backpack and pulled out the envelope full of cash. It was time to get a cab.

"Where to?" the driver asked when she got in.

"Santa Monica," Roach said with all the confidence she could conjure.

The driver looked at her through the rearview mirror, but didn't move. Roach met his eyes and tightened her lips like she was done with the topic.

"Address?" he said.

Roach tried not to crack and recited the address on the envelope from memory.

He nodded, said something in a language she didn't recognize and then muttered, "Fuckin' rich kids," loud enough for her to hear.

Roach would've told him to fuck off, but she was on foreign terrain. She concentrated her energy, instead, on appearing to be someone at home.

The taxi wove in and out of city streets, passing more of what Roach had seen, but from inside the cab, things seemed bigger, making the city feel different. She fixated on these differences to try to distract from her nervousness. She worried, again, that somehow her mom might be near. Like maybe she might appear in Santa Monica to meet her as soon as the taxi dropped her off. She'd be so quiet, for so long, and then eventually she'd ask Roach why she ever thought any of this dumb stuff would work. Roach wouldn't have an answer. Even if she did, what would be the point of telling her mom? She wanted to leave her, to leave everything. She was sick of El Valle. She had dreams. Night was falling, she was getting anxious.

Suddenly, it was like someone turned on the LA fantasy that had previously only existed in her head. Down the street from a lit-up pier, the crimson-orange sun sank into the ocean horizon, and things felt more like what Roach anticipated. She craned her neck to get as much of the view as she could for as long as she could. A few turns later, the driver said, "Okay," and Roach looked out her window and saw a small, colorless house. The lights inside were all off. It didn't feel real. She looked along the street to both ends of the block where they were and then back to the driver.

"Ninety dollars," he said without hesitation.

She reached into her backpack, took out five twenty-dollar bills, but stopped just short of handing them over.

"Do you know if there are, like, any cheap motels nearby?" she said and flashed her teeth nervously.

The driver made a sound like he was forcing something out of his throat. Suddenly, he turned around and grabbed for Roach's wrist, but she was too quick for him. She braced herself and sat back as far as she could against her seat.

The driver threw his hands in the air and looked at Roach. "I'm not a motel. I don't know about motel. You wanted to come to Santa Monica, I brought you." Then he clapped to punctuate his words. "Give me my fare! You want a motel? Go call a motel!"

As he kept clapping and waving his hands around, Roach, wordless, breathless, dropped the crumpled five bills onto the seat. She grabbed her bags, opened the cab door and stepped out into the California dusk. Even after the driver volleyed a few more insults at her and the cab peeled out, she was in a haze. She'd made it, but what the hell did that even mean? Maybe she'd turn on her phone and call her mom, just to prove her ability to plan and follow through. *Hey mom, I successfully ran away before you even noticed. And guess what? I totally know the person sending you money is . . .* Roach kept herself from completing the fantasy. She knew, or thought she knew, who it was that sent them money. But when she played out the exchange with her mom in her mind, she always went blank when the money's source was revealed. The moment at which she found herself was an emptiness she didn't know how to fill. Fear crept into her body.

The ocean breeze cut through her hoodie and made her shiver. She hadn't moved since exiting the cab and stepping onto the sidewalk. She took a few steps in one direction and then turned toward the sea, to where the sun disappeared. Out of nowhere a shadowed figure walked her way. She stared at it and wondered whether she should move away or ask them for help.

As it got closer, the figure turned out to be an older man in a full-body wetsuit, a light blueish-gray surfboard under his arm. Roach stared at him.

"Do you know who lives here?" she blurted, motioning with her head.

The old man said nothing.

Suddenly, she was in a standoff, and her shivering might give away something about herself she needed to hide. She tried to steady herself.

Without a word, the old man slowly reached up to his ash-colored beard and scratched absent-mindedly. Then his hand returned to his side. He cleared his throat, but only more silence followed. Then he snorted, turned and walked toward the side of the house. All of his movements seemed carefree, insults showing Roach how little she mattered.

"Wait," Roach said, relaxing a bit without this stranger's gaze directly on her. "Is that it? I asked you a question, man."

She felt her body heating up. The streetlamps had come on, and her eyes adjusted to the night lighting. With the return of her sight came the reminder that she was hundreds of miles from anything familiar. She wasn't going to be deterred by this old weirdo—even if he might be her dad. She followed him to the side of the house. Without looking at her, he set his surfboard up against a fence, walked over to an outdoor shower and began rinsing himself off.

Roach watched him from a safe distance. She hadn't expected a warm welcome, but she wouldn't let herself be treated like she was nothing either. This guy owed her an explanation, if nothing else.

"Hey, anytime you feel like acknowledging a fellow human being," she said. "I'll be here. No rush, surfer bro."

Finally, the old man shut the water off, shook out his stringy, gray hair and beard, turned to Roach and said, "All right, dudette, I'm fully de-salted. What can I do ya for?"

There was a softness to his voice, as if Roach had known him her whole life. His wet face glowed in the orange light of the streetlamp.

"This your place?" Roach said, feeling more like herself. It was business time.

The old man chuckled. "This my place, all right. What's it to you?"

Roach didn't have a follow-up beyond, "Nothing." She didn't know how to proceed.

The old man's smile faded. He shook his head, turned and walked towards the back of the house.

Roach panicked. "Julia Mitchell in El Valle, Arizona!" she shouted at his back.

He stopped.

Oh shit, she thought, shit shit shit shit shit.

He turned and studied her, his face tightening.

Roach fought to keep herself from trembling, to stand firm and meet his gaze. She approached him with slow but deliberate steps.

She swallowed, preparing herself for flight. "She's my mom."

The old man's eyes got big. She felt safe enough to look down into her backpack and take out the letter with the address of the house on it.

"You send us money, every month," she said, holding the envelope in front of her like a lantern. Then said, "Dad."

"Ah, shit," the old man said and stepped towards her.

In the full glow of the streetlamp, Roach studied his eyes, his shoulders rising and slumping in a sigh.

"It's not you, is it?" she said, embarrassed by the fragility of her own voice.

* * *

"Well, shit, where do we start?" he said to Roach as she took a seat across from him in his living room. "I guess you can call me grandpa. . . . "

Roach dubbed him "Gramps" in her mind.

Neither of them spoke for what felt like an eternity. Suddenly, he looked around the living room, as though he had misplaced something important.

"You know what? Hang on. I gotta get . . . " He got up and walked out of the room.

In his absence, Roach took in the decor. All over the walls were images of tiny surfers on the brink of being swallowed by enormous ocean waves. There were also framed black-and-white posters of guys with slicked-back hair, wearing matching suits and holding guitars. Each seemed to be advertising a different show: *Back to Skankin'! For One Night Only: Dick Dale and his Deltones! Drummin' Eddie and Strummin' Freddie: The Oahu Brothers Together Again!*

They all looked like they hadn't been touched in years. Roach felt a mix of adrenaline and hunger. She scanned the room, just in case she might have to make a quick get-away. She hadn't let herself totally believe her father was on the other end of the checks, but, still, she wished any part of the room felt more familiar or instinctual.

She noticed one photo, on the far end of the room, sitting next to a record player, but just then Gramps came back. He carried a black, square case, which he set down in front of the record player. He had changed into a pair of khaki cargo shorts and a short-sleeve floral print shirt. His gray-white hair was tucked beneath a bright yellow knit cap. His glasses rested on the tip of his nose. Yup, if I were gonna have a grandpa, Roach thought, this is the model the manufacturer would send.

Gramps placed the needle down onto a record he'd gotten out of the case. The speakers scratched for a moment before a steady drumbeat faded in, followed by guitar riffs. Roach's eyes caught Gramps' gaze, and he smiled. He walked back to his place across from where she sat. Roach stayed on guard, in case she needed to jump out a window or something. She smiled at Gramps as he pulled his chair up to the coffee table between them, reached into his breast pocket and pulled out a baggie of marijuana and a small, wooden pipe.

"All right, dudette. Now we can make like family and really get this reunion going," he said as he took a whiff of the weed in the baggie. "Wooh! Real fresh family." He laughed, and, as he packed the pipe, she took the chance to ask one of the billion questions she had.

"So, uh, 'Gramps,'" she said, making finger quotes just in case her new old family member found the title undesirable. He didn't seem to mind. "You got yourself one hell of a spot here, so I gotta ask, how do you afford it, you know, living near the beach and sending us money and all?"

Roach knew you're never supposed to talk money with family, but money was the only real connection between her and Gramps. They couldn't talk about anything else. Plus, as she watched her grandfather pack a pipe with weed, she concluded social norms weren't for them.

She waited. He finished packing the bowl, flicked the lighter's flame over it for a second, inhaled and said, "The luck of the cosmic draw." He held his breath for a moment then exhaled, coughing.

"You know the citrus or strawberries you see in grocery stores?" he said between coughs.

Confused, Roach considered the riddle. Her exhaustion was catching up to her, so she looked at Gramps and shrugged.

He took another short puff and exhaled. "Sorry. Wasn't a trick question," he said, voice high-pitched. He exhaled. "My folks, uh, your great-grand folks, founded a farm north of here about ninety years ago. Oranges, lemons, strawberries, grapefruits . . . " He waved his hands. "You get it. Anyway, when those fruits need to be had in stores, the Northern Valley Fruit Co. is who they call."

"So, you're in charge of the farms now?"

Gramps shook his head. He leaned forward, offering her the pipe. She took it.

"Sure, my name's technically on the board, but I ain't been by any of it since after Mary, uh, your grandma, I mean, passed, and then when Julia . . . " He stopped himself and suddenly looked surprised to see Roach. He whistled to fill the dead air and tried to refocus his attention on the pipe in Roach's hand. "You, uh, gonna hit that, or what?" he said

Roach obliged, hoping to gain his trust and hear more.

Moments later, Roach was floating on the smoke between her and Gramps. The music rushed and receded like the waves outside, and Gramps told stories of hitchhiking up and down the coast, trading grass for transport, sneaking into surf rock shows and, one time, filling in on drums for a lowly three-dude group playing in a Bay Area dive bar.

"Didn't know a tom-tom from my own asshole!" he shouted, and they both laughed.

Roach could barely breathe. She felt like she had to clutch the couch beneath her, or she might float away like a balloon and pop.

"Aww, man," Gramps said and passed the pipe back to Roach. "Yeah, I really had to rein it in when I met your grandma, though. 'Georgie baby.'" Gramps lightened his voice. "Mary'd say to me, 'When are we going to ditch these scenes and get ourselves a nice pad? Just you, me and whoever else might surprise us?'" He laughed and wiped his eyes.

As he got up to change the record, Roach collected herself and took another hit, even though she already felt over-inflated. "No shit," she said. "God, why the hell didn't mom ever tell me any of this? I don't know why she's so goddamned secretive about you or my dad."

"Well, I mean your pop's a whole 'nother saga," Gramps said over his shoulder and fumbled with the record he was trying to play. He finally got the record on the turntable and placed the needle on the disk carefully. Within seconds the room was filled with long guitar sounds and drums building to—something terrible, Roach thought. She suddenly wanted quiet. When Gramps came back to his seat and reached for his pipe, she pulled her hand away.

"What do you mean by 'a whole 'nother saga?'" she said and got up.

Gramps looked up but said nothing.

Roach walked on weightless legs to the record player and lowered the volume. She looked back at Gramps.

Gramps sighed. "Listen, little dudette, uh, Roxy. I'm not really here to say anything definitively. Last I knew of Marco, he'd had a tough run-in with the law. His status in the country being complicated, ya know?"

Absent-mindedly, Roach turned the music back up and closed her eyes. She couldn't remember ever hearing the name of her father before. *Marco*. The name bounced and crested against every corner of her mind. It wasn't a name that sounded like a man but more like a kid's knickname—the name of someone in over his head, too far from home.

Gramps came over to where she stood and turned the music back up. Then, he put a hand on her shoulder and grabbed the pipe with his other hand. He spoke as he walked back to his seat, facing away.

"Julia really leaned on him after she found out she was pregnant. Then your grandma passed. It was all too much, ya know?" Roach heard Gramps as though he were on the other side of a tunnel. "Everything happened all at once and. . . . " She heard him puff from the pipe and cough. The music getting louder.

"What the fuck does that even mean?" Roach groaned. "What the fuck does any of that mean?"

Gramps just exhaled and coughed again.

Roach looked at the photo near the record player. She recognized Gramps and guessed the woman at his side was her grandma. They smiled and stood in front of a parked VW van. To their left was a younger woman, unmistakably Roach's mom, Julia, in a sundress. She was also smiling. Next to her, with his arm around her waist, was a young man in jeans and a white T-shirt. His eyes, his hair, his nose—she was looking at herself in another life, a life she knew nothing about. She wanted answers.

"What happened to him?"

Gramps, still with his back to her, said, "Deported."

Roach was shaking. "What?"

"Yup." Gramps sighed and turned towards Roach. "Your grandma passed, and Julia and me just couldn't seem to see eye-to-eye on things with her gone. Then she found out she was pregnant and . . . well, she convinced Marco to head south with her. Folks at that time were warned about the checkpoints. The whole scene here in California had gotten real ugly, ya know? The same kinda ugliness that always seems to infect this place just when honest folks seem to be making headway in the country. And it wasn't like it was Marco's fault, ya know? Dude came over with his folks when he was real little. They passed before he had a chance to apply for any kinda permanent residence with them. So, along the way to Arizona, they got stopped. He just didn't have all his papers in order . . . " Gramps blew out the resin from the pipe. He reached into the bag to pack another bowl.

Roach, still shaking, walked over to the couch with the photo in hand. She began to feel like her eyes were boiling inside her skull. Don't do it, she told herself fighting tears, don't fucking do it. She did.

"What did you do to help?" she said, barely getting the words out.

Gramps kept his head down and shrugged.

"What could I do? Julia and I'd had a rough go of it after Mary passed. If she hadn't told me months after that she was keeping her baby, I maybe never would've heard from her again." He finished packing the pipe and was going to take a hit, still not looking at Roach.

She reached out to grab the pipe. She bumped Gramps' hands and sent weed scattering.

"But weren't you ever curious?" she said, still fighting tears. "You knew where we lived. You knew about me and about my dad. You never thought about coming to visit or trying to help him or getting his stuff in order or . . . or, or anything?" She felt an urge to break something.

Gramps shrugged. "People gotta walk their own paths." His voice was calm but not as warm as it had been. "Julia made her choice. Plus, after Mary . . . I-I just couldn't, ya know?"

Roach felt the world turning against her will, spinning as though to eject her. She hated that he wasn't yelling. She wanted him to yell. *She* wanted to yell, wanted to drown the room the way the music had.

"We struggle, you know?" Roach said. "Mom and I always fight about money and other stupid shit. And all this time, you could've been helping us out. Helping *me* out." She tugged at her hoodie with both hands.

Gramps dropped his head, then lifted it suddenly and looked her in the eyes. His faded green pupils suddenly sharp, contrasted against redness. His body swelled.

"Listen, kid, I hate to harsh your vibes, but you don't know how any of this works, all right?"

Roach tried to keep herself steady, but she felt dizzy. She saw black rings framing every part of the room and stumbled back onto the couch.

"Unless this is what you came here to do. To get mad at some old dude burning through his inheritance before he croaks all alone in his pad. . . . " He coughed out the last of the sentence. "And the army of lawyers find a way to leach as much of it as they can for themselves."

Roach shook her head. She tried but couldn't bring her vision back into focus. She wanted to fight Gramps, to show him she wasn't a newcomer to arguments, that she wasn't someone to cross, but "whatever" was all she managed to say.

"You want some grandfatherly advice?" Gramps yelled. "Don't ever assume you've lost more than anyone you meet. Pain ain't something you measure against others, you got that?"

Roach's head wasn't floating anymore, it was heavy and careening towards earth. She felt like she needed her mom there, to counter what Gramps was saying, but also to catch her. She tried reaching out toward Gramps, but she dropped the photo— it hit the ground with a galactic thud.

"Woah, little dudette. Are you all right?" Gramps said, his voice miles away.

Everything went blank, silent.

* * *

Roach woke up.

She was lying on the couch where she'd passed out. The curtains in the living room were too thick for her to know what time it was, but through the slightly opened windows she could hear gulls outside. This she took to mean night had passed. Her head throbbed. She felt a heavy emptiness in her body. She got out from under a blanket that had somehow found its way onto her. The previous night came back: Gramps, the surf, Dad, deported, Mom, El Valle.

She was sweating. She took off her hoodie, sat up and smelled food. Her stomach growled. From instinct, she stood and walked to the kitchen.

Gramps was sifting through the records, in a different case on the table. Next to his case was a plate of hash browns, scrambled eggs and a glass of orange juice. My legacy, Roach thought, and snorted a little.

Gramps looked up from his records, startled. He was still in last night's clothes. Roach wondered if he'd slept at all.

"Oh. Hey, little dudette," he said with a raspy voice. He cleared his throat but kept his voice quiet. "Figured you'd have a mean appetite, ya know, if you made it through the night." He laughed nervously.

Roach joined him. Morbid joking about her death was something, oddly, that she had always wanted in a grandfather.

"Should probably do this away from here," Gramps said. He lifted the case, turned and walked towards a counter. "Don't wanna get dust on you or your chow," he said over his shoulder.

From behind he looked like an aged, gray badger rummaging lethargically through a familiar trash can. Roach sat at the table. She picked at the eggs and hash browns with her fork before saying, "Hey, uh, Gramps . . . "

He stopped his rummaging but didn't turn around. "Yeah?" He said, sounding scared.

"You got any Tapatío for these eggs? I hate to be picky, but, you know, I just found out I'm half-Mexican, so I wanna make sure I'm doing my heritage proud." She forced a laugh.

This time it was Gramps who helped ease her by laughing along. He turned to her with a smile. "Oh, hell yeah, dudette. No worries, I got all the hot sauces you could ever want and more," he said with an energy Roach recognized from last night.

Roach ate most of the breakfast, with little else said between her and Gramps.

As they sat across one another at his table, she finally asked. "What do you think Mom's doing with the money?"

"Beats me," he said and shrugged.

Roach reached into her pocket and took her phone out. She took a deep breath. "Well, I guess there's only one way to find out, right? She turned it on and saw she had missed calls and texts from her mom. She turned to look at Gramps.

"I mean, either you or me; somebody's gotta call," he said, "and I'd bet she's way more in the mood to hear from you."

They chuckled at this, like kids who knew they weren't in too much trouble.

Roach pressed the button to call her mom. One ring. Then a scared voice said, "Roxana?"

"Yeah, Mom. It's me."

Then silence, or so Roach thought. After a few seconds, she could hear her mom crying quietly on the other end. Jesus, she thought, all of this *for me*?

"Mom, it's okay. I'm okay. I promise. Guess what? It turns out Grandpa and I get along great. Who'd've guessed? The power of genes, huh?" She forced a smile at Gramps.

He smiled back and gave her two thumbs up.

Her mom's crying slowed down. She could hear her breathing. "Roxana," she said, her voice soft rain on glass, "I'm sorry I never told you. I never thought I would keep it secret forever, but I . . . I didn't know how to begin to tell you. I'm so sorry."

"It's all right," Roach said. "It's all right, Mom. Really, it's all right."

Silence on her mom's end.

"Mom? Can we talk about it now?"

Her mom inhaled deeply. Again. Again. Finally, she said, "Yes, Roxana."

* * *

The sights outside the Greyhound window made Roach's insides churn. Nothing about the people or the roads was off-putting, but Roach didn't know how she had made it so far from home, and she couldn't imagine going farther still. Her pulse spiked every time the bus lurched forward only to stop suddenly. She looked again at the photo of her mother, her father and her grandparents; the one she had taken from Gramps' place. Her thoughts crashed and rolled into themselves like waves on the Santa Monica beach. When the bus stopped, finally at the border, the ocean in her mind crested. The driver came over the loudspeaker and instructed the passengers, first in English then in Spanish, to gather their belongings to be checked by customs and to meet back on the bus once they had all been cleared to enter Tijuana. Roach put the photograph in her backpack, with care, next to the envelope with cash from Gramps and the piece of paper with an address and phone number she'd gotten from her mom.

Melissa Gets Out

I was convinced this couldn't be happening, that I'd never actually get out. We sat there: not moving along with every other car in rush hour traffic. Just me and my dad in his truck with no air conditioning or a working stereo.

How did I so perfectly predict how much this would suck?

I swear it's my only real gift: to know full-well how much I'm about to unnecessarily suffer to do a basic thing. I mean, people leave for college all the time. I see it happening in so many dumb movies and TV shows, and I read all the headlines celebrating brown kids who make it to college. But, when *I* try, the world goes, "Hold up, girl. Your road outta here has to be hella annoying." The angrier I got, the less we moved. I hated everything and everyone. I hated my hometown for making getting out so hard. I hated my new college for giving me money for tuition but not plane fare. I hated how my mom had said, "*Tu papá* will drive you to school, Melissa, *ya deja de fregar!*" sentencing me to a sixteen-hour car ride with my less-than-talkative dad. Most of all, I hated myself, knowing I wouldn't be able to hate these other things much longer.

I sighed and looked over at my dad. He seemed completely unaffected, as usual, by anything. I briefly thought about trying to make small talk, but I abandoned it just as quickly. If he and I hadn't had anything to say to each other in eighteen years together, why act brand new? I'd spent my whole life only ever getting one-word or grunt answers to my questions. At best, he might say, "Go ask your *amá*," so without her around, I knew better. Some people are talkers and some people are Mexican dads who nod and shrug their way through parenting. I didn't hold this against him, but I didn't totally like it either.

So instead of talking, I sank into my seat, put earbuds in, turned up my music, put my sunglasses on, closed my eyes and let my anxious energy rot into exhaustion.

When I awoke, my sunglasses made the dark blue desert and purple sky feel even darker and endless. I took them off and saw our headlights cutting through the land ahead. My music had died. Wind slashing against the truck was the only sound I heard. I stretched and yawned. Then I turned to Dad. He was just as I'd left him.

Before I could speak, he said, "We're in *Nuevo México.*"

"Uhum."

"Tu *mamá* called. I told her you were asleep, *que todo 'stá bien.*"

"Already?" I looked straight ahead, puffed my cheeks and sighed at the prospect of this new normal. "*Esa mujer.* She's gotta relax. I can't handle this kinda helicoptering for the next four years."

"*Así es tu mamá,*" Dad said and cleared his throat.

A moment passed and then he spoke again. Damn. Two full sentences back to back!

"With our history here, she's afraid of what can happen, especially when someone is far from home."

His first few words rang in my mind: *our history here.* I always knew mom worried way too much about most stuff, especially me. It's normal. Mexican moms worry for their daughters because they don't think we can do things for ourselves, especially in a country they don't totally understand. I knew the truth, though. I knew I'd busted my ass to get into college and to get the whole thing pretty much paid for with scholarships. For all his non-talkativeness, at least my dad gave me space. Mom said all the time about him, "*Así es de campesino tu papá*," which meant he was from a way more rural part of México than she was, but I always understood her words to mean my dad wasn't bothered by the wider world around or within him as long as it didn't mess with his day-to-day life.

Maybe this was why suddenly hearing him talk about their history caught me by surprise. I knew my parents had a life before me. I didn't think of them as having "history," though, especially one that would make them afraid of uncertainty. Except for . . .

"Apá," I said, "are we close to where Pedrito died?"

His face didn't change its expression. The same stern look glowed and went dark as we passed lights on the highway. He rubbed below his eyes, stretching the skin taut against his cheekbones, his scruff bristling against his fingers. He cleared his throat but still didn't say anything. We sat there like strangers forced to share a space with all pleasantries exhausted. I worried I'd upset him. Had I waited too long to be curious about my brother? Was it just that my dad was tired?

In the vacuum of silence, I closed my eyes and conjured the photo of Pedrito on the dresser in my parents' bedroom. Taken when he was a baby, four years before I was born, in the photo his tiny eyes are nearly closed by his cheeks puffed up in a smile. Mom went to church every year on his birthday to light a candle and to tell him about our lives. Sometimes, like when guys playing ball in the park would cat-call at me as I walked home from school, or when teachers at school would be surprised by the quality of my work—praise in the form of having overwhelmed their low expectations—I wondered how much having an older brother would've helped. Someone to make me feel like I wasn't doing this alone. I tried to imagine what we might talk about and what kinds of things he would've done with our mom so she wouldn't make me her all-or-nothing.

* * *

After we stopped in El Paso to refuel, get food and use the bathroom, I resigned myself to the silence in the truck. We were just out of the city limits, however, before my dad finally answered what I had asked earlier.

"It was *por aquí*, just east of El Paso," he said, waving a hand across the windshield. "*Tu mamá* and I had finally gotten residency, *gracias al hijo-de-su-madre* Reagan, and we were coming back from visiting her family in Monterrey. It was our first time back in México since our wedding."

I'd forgotten, my parents had spent the first seven years of their time here without papers. All the while, they were so close—within driving distance—to their homes and their families, but they couldn't go see them.

"*Tu mamá* never thought we would stay in this country for very long. She always wanted to return *a nuestra tierra* when it was time to start our own family," he said. "Then Pedrito was born here, a citizen. With how things were in México, we thought about how Pedrito could live and work here instead. He could go to school and maybe have more than we could give him in our land. He could build a home." Dad sighed.

"And then?" I could barely hear myself over the wind or the tires on the road.

"*Pues.*" Dad cleared his throat. "Pedrito was sixteen months old when we finally got papers. We went to Monterrey for a few days, so he could meet your *tíos* and *tías* and *tus abuelos—que descansen en paz*—and . . . *pues* . . . we were coming back late at night because *tu mamá* had to get back to work, *y. . . .* "

I knew. Although he'd never been much of a conversationalist, Dad did tell me stories when I was a little girl. Mom, too. They both had told me about this night. I pictured them driving in the opposite direction on I-10. Pedrito between them in a car seat, cooing, staring forward at the windshield. Was he awake when the drunk driver hit their car? Did he hear our parents' voices as they cried and begged for help? The scene played out—projected before me on the same desert where my family had once driven in a different life . . . until it faded into nothing.

I inhaled hard, congested suddenly. Dad was still talking, but I could barely hear him. I hadn't realized, but I was crying. I tried to hide my tears, but I think Dad heard me. I felt his hand on my shoulder. It was warmth I didn't know I still needed. I went towards it, instinctively, and sobbed until I was asleep again.

* * *

This time Dad woke me up. We were near San Antonio. I opened the window and tasted the air and hoped it would nourish me. He handed me a breakfast burrito he'd picked up at some place while I slept. Neither of us said anything.

We remained silent when we got to campus. Dad helped me move my things up the asphalt walk, up the small stoop, through the two hallways, to my dorm room. Once we finished, sweating and panting a little, I walked with him back to his truck. I thought about maybe seeing if he wanted to grab food in town, but I was ready to be on my own. Dad must've been ready, too, I thought.

"Okay, *m'ija*," he said, finally, the bags under his eyes tender. He cleared his throat and shrugged. "*Te cuidas*, yeah?"

"Okay, *Apá*." I smiled and hugged him

He hugged me back.

He got into his truck, started the engine, gave me a wave as he pulled out of the parking lot and back towards the highway. I stood in the humid, sun-soaked afternoon, watched until there wasn't anything left to watch and then let my imagination put my dad closer to our home.

To Live & Die in EV

Cop cars surround Washington Park when you get home. Crane your head, try to see what's up. But you can't. Too many cops, too much history. Walk into your house, see your mom in the living room. *Salúdala.* Tell her school was all right, that you went to a friend's house afterwards to hang out. Hope she doesn't notice your toxic scent or shifting gaze. Ask her what happened at the park. She just got home from working in other people's homes, cleaning other people's messes, so she doesn't know. You try to paint the scene for her but can't.

"*Ve tú.* See for yourself," you finally say.

She sighs with all the years she's lived in this land, gets up from her chair and walks outside to investigate—her sore feet caressed by *chanclas* purchased in a *mercado* in another life. She no longer says to your old man, "*Viejo,* let's get out of El Valle," because they've cycled too many times through the same back-and-forths and inescapable truths. Besides, everyone says the hood isn't as bad as it used to be.

In the front yard, your mom can't see much of what's happening in the park. She waves across the street at Raquelle, your boy Josiah's mom, who waves back and shrugs. Then, Raquelle's eyes widen when an ambulance screams past them.

Raquelle babysat a lot of the kids in the neighborhood, including you. This is how you became friends with her only son, Josiah. Y'all would lay on your stomachs and watch TV while

Raquelle sat in the kitchen, waiting for the phone to ring and bring news of another denied parole. She'd mourn again a life that wouldn't stop ending. Then she'd send y'all outside to play Power Rangers or Ninja Turtles or any game where y'all could fight each other without the need for winners and losers.

Josiah grew up, and Raquelle found new men, but none stuck. When she had to work twice as much to make it for her and Josiah, that's when him and y'all would spend more time at Washington Park. He got long and fast and confident enough to take on anyone one-on-one on the basketball courts.

"Josiah-in-your-eye-uh," you called him: great on his own, decent with teammates.

Your cousin Sergio, lanky, stubborn and a sore loser, wanted another piece of him.

"Ey, Josiah," Sergio said, after he played solid defense but still got scored on, "you keep it up, you'll have almost as many buckets as stepdaddies."

Josiah stopped, shoved Sergio with a "Fuck you say, bitch?" and had to be held back.

Then everyone started shouting: about daddies and stepdaddies and mommas and *mamás* and sisters and cousins until the wrong person yelled the wrong shit and fists detonated.

"Why the fuck you always doin' this?" Another of your cousins yelled at Sergio afterwards. The cops had been called and everybody fled to different houses, complaining about *those other people* and *their* violence.

Sergio laughed because he had nothing else. His dad had been deported earlier that year, and his mom had stopped going to work because she feared she was next. Your parents and other *tías* and *tíos* were supporting them. Sergio even stopped showing up to classes at Desertwood High School so he could help, too. He started by giving half his check to his mom and using the other half for escape—the kind that was processed, bagged, bought and sold in alleys. After not too long, though, he wasn't even giving his mom half. She was suddenly a foreigner dependent on the mercy of a citizen and didn't know how to ask for more.

"Man," Sergio said, "you fuckin' *putos* don't know shit about bein' *for real* afraid." He laughed until chemical coughing consumed him.

Then your *tía* came into the living room and told y'all that the cops had left the park. Y'all sat there, puffed lips, swollen eyes, sweat-stenched, shaking your heads, until Sergio said, "Somebody call up Indio. See if he's at home right now. See if he's got that hookup."

Somebody did.

His real name is Juan and he lives on the Salt River Pima-Maricopa Rez to the north. People from the hood go and kick it there because it's like freedom, but, like, fake freedom, like knock-off, store-brand shit you can buy on the cheap.

Juan and some other O'odham dudes used to come ball in Washington Park. Back when y'all were still too young to understand territory and loss. Elbows and knees flew as Juan and his boys ran up and down the court. Because they were Indian, some of you called their play dirty. So, after some shit-talking, some shoving and another brawl broken up by cops, they stopped coming altogether.

Some of you went to them instead. Playing ball, at first, then smoking, drinking, crushing, snorting and shooting after. Time passed differently on their rez. In the hood, you forgot you were in a desert, forgot you were surviving where no one was supposed to. You thought you were strength. You thought your survival meant something.

Then one of Juan's uncles brought up the White Man and said, "Man, survival ain't shit but trading buckets and never catchin' up. It ain't a game you can ever win." He killed a beer and walked outside to smoke. Left y'all there to sit in emptiness.

Walking back in your hood, you head towards your house and think about white people: the ones in school, the ones in office, the ones in uniform. They put Juan on a rez and told him it was Manifest Destiny. They raided the landscaping company where your *tío* worked and deported him, leaving your *tía* to figure shit out. They put Raquelle's man in chains and tortured him with a freedom he'd never be pure enough to earn. They harassed and threatened and warred and turned up the heat on all y'all until nothing was left but for Sergio and Josiah to break each other open in a park where kids play.

Tourista

I'd gone out drinking the night before, even though I had class the following morning at 10, so I was asleep when the phone rang at about 3 p.m., and I stumbled over to where my roommate and I had put the landline in our dorm room and answered "Huh?" and from the other side heard a voice asking if I was me, and I still didn't know what was happening but I grunted to show that I was, and the voice said, "This is Mark in the admissions office, we have a student and his father who want a tour of the campus," and I recognized the words but still didn't know what was happening because I didn't work for the admissions office, had never taken a tour and had only been a student for two months; I looked out the window at the New England fall foliage—which still felt new—to corroborate this, but, somehow, I said, "Uh-huh" and Mark, who may've been a student or just someone from town working for this rich, private college, said, "Well, they're Mexican, and they want a Mexican tour guide, and . . ." (I'm not omitting anything Mark said, or didn't say, I guess, he stopped himself mid-sentence, before he could utter what had slapped me in the face when I first got to campus: there are no Mexicans, or, there hadn't been, I guess; that Fall, people like Mark could now say, *Yes, we have someone who we can call up, just a minute please*), so maybe it was because I missed my family, missed my hood, missed El Valle, or maybe it was some sense of obligation I felt to the school for funding my escape from those things, or maybe I was just down, hungover and lonely, but I said, "Yeah, I'll head over," hung up the phone, walked to the bathroom down the hall, washed my face and left my dorm headed in the direction of the first Mexicans I'd seen in months, who were, when I got there, as advertised, a father and son—both unmistakably brown but definitely whiter than I'd pictured, but our hair and eyes could be traded and no one would know the difference—and they smiled when they saw me, said, "Hello nice to meet you" and then "*un placer*" once I let them know I was the kind of Mexican American who spoke *Spanish* Spanish, not just *cholo* Spanglish but the type of Spanish that professors cared about, the type of Spanish (I've since learned) is necessary for going through customs or other checkpoints, but nowhere else in the world, but I didn't know this then, so when the father (whose name I've since forgotten) said "*Órale, vámonos en nuestro tour*," I laughed from familiarity and unease, and we began our tour by walking to the student union and then to the humanities building, which I knew the most about but also knew next to nothing about because, like I said, it was my first semester in college and I hadn't learned enough to tell anyone why it was better or worse than any other college, I wasn't even sure whether it was better than the hood—no, I'm trippin', it was definitely better than the hood, but I couldn't really say *why*—and, anyway, Jonás, (that was the kid's name) was interested in doing something pre-med, so eventually he asked "Can we go to the science building then?" and I said, "*Claro que sí*," and on the walk across the quad, I pointed up the hill to the library and said *biblioteca* and waited for both of them to acknowledge my tour guide action, Jonás' dad asked "*¿Y qué onda con las chicas?*" with his head tilted down, eyes looking over glasses, as a group of white girls (definitely upperclassmen) walked past us, and I laughed to show I understood and said, "Lotsa really smart, pretty girls here," and Jonás' dad nudged Jonás with the back of his hand and wheeze-laughed while Jonás smiled and turned crimson, then we were at the science building—a place I'd never been, so didn't say much about—and we walked past classrooms and labs before sitting in one of the lounges to talk about other things: "*¿Naciste en México?*" Jonás' dad asked and I told him I hadn't but both of my parents had, "*¿Y de dónde son tus padres?*" he asked and I said, "*Mi amá es de Monterrey, Nuevo León*" to which he nodded, approving, and said, "One of my sisters lives there; *¡una ciudad maravillosa!*" and I smiled and said "And *mi apá es un Rarámuri de Batopilas, Chihuahua*," and his smile disappeared into his face like a window slamming shut, and things got quiet, but after a few moments, he managed to say, "I've never been to the Sierra in Chihuahua, or really to any *pueblo de indios;* those places are . . . not for us" and I turned to Jonás, who looked at the ground, so I started saying, "You should" but stopped; my words hitting the floor in front of me like vomit or blood from an open wound; neither of them looked at me, and I realized no answer I gave could make it sound like I hadn't cheated my way to a place I didn't belong, and I tried to tell myself I hadn't and that I wasn't embarrassed and didn't care what these fools thought, so I said I had to get back to work and it was good getting to know them; I wished Jonás luck because I felt like we hadn't really talked and he seemed like a nice enough kid, and his dad shook my hand professionally, disinterested and said, "*Muchas gracias, muchacho,*" and I nodded the way I would to a stranger—an older one, expecting nothing of me or my kind—and I walked back to my dorm thinking about my parents and the weight of their hometowns, until my mouth felt dry with fear, so I texted a friend to see where there would be beer later and waited for night to fall.

Cut & Fade

The summer heat tried to punish me for coming back, but I was barely sweating by the time I got to Alex's. I had to ring a few times before he finally answered the door, wearing a pair of basketball shorts and nothing else. He'd just woken up. The tattoo he'd gotten when he was in high school of our last name—*Aguirre*—sagged on his abdomen as though it also needed more time to wake up. It was 2 p.m.

* * *

I'd moved away for school and stayed away for work—and for my girlfriend. I hadn't been back in EV in almost four years, hadn't seen my cousin Alex in nearly five. Still, once I knew I was visiting, I held off on getting a haircut because I wanted it cut the way I used to get it back in the day.

I repeated motions I hadn't performed since I was a teenager. We dapped, hugged. I pulled off my T-shirt as we walked towards his bathroom and I sat on his toilet while he pulled his kit out from beneath the sink. I was back.

"All right, dogg," he said, still wiping sleep from his eyes. "How do you want it?"

"Same as always, cuz." I lifted my right hand to my head and ran my fingers through my hair. "Tight on the sides, scissors up top, and fade it in."

He nodded, cleared his throat and turned on his clippers.

He started with the left side of my head. The clippers struggled at first to get through the thick growth I'd cultivated over the past year. So many times I'd had to fend off Sarah, tell her I was waiting to be back in my hometown to cut my hair. I told her it was just how we did things in my neighborhood, how I'd done it for most of my life.

"It's just getting out of control," she said. "You've gotten it cut around here tons of times, haven't you? Why can't you just find somebody in town to do it?"

I didn't want to fight, so I didn't push back. I didn't tell her how, most of the time, I just trimmed my own hair—with varying results—and hid it under a cap all winter. I didn't mention how she probably didn't notice because of all the traveling she was doing for work to Boston or New York or DC. I didn't bring up the one time I actually went to a barber in Portland and the old white guy nodded like he knew what I'd asked for. He ran the clippers through different parts of my head and asked, "That good?" Then shrugged and kept cutting after I had said, "No."

Remembering that sent waves of embarrassment through me for weeks after. I told Sarah she wouldn't understand and that there wasn't anything more to talk about.

I could feel the left side of my head breathe, and part of me wanted to stop right then and go outside to let the hot wind kiss it.

"So how you been, man?" I asked Alex.

"Been all right." His words were muffled and distorted by the buzz-humming so close to my ear. "Work at the hotel is kinda slow right now, but that's always how it is. Tourists only mess with AZ when they can handle the weather, you know? It's just how life is for us."

"Well, hey, man, it's good to be back," I said and forced a laugh into the air.

He chuckled and cleared his throat. "For sure, dogg. It's good to have you back." He motioned for me to turn so he could move to the back of my head. "Good you come to see the family and to be home for minute, you know? You gotta stay close to your roots. Not like these wack-ass tourists, buncha old farts. They don't come here for anything real, you know? And they don't come from anywhere real, either. It sounds crazy but that's how I see it."

My chin was pressed to my chest, but I mustered an "uh huh."

He moved the clippers away from the back of my head.

"Like, if all you do is show up to some place, act like you own it, treat it like everyone and everything work for you, and then just disappear and forget all about us, then we ain't want you. Period. You know?" His tone was calm, and he didn't raise his voice, but I sensed a change, like I could hear his pulse rising.

"It's good to see my mom again," I said, trying to avoid whatever rant was coming.

"Word."

That's it. That was all he offered. I stared at the wall and thought about Sarah and me. We'd planned to take our vacation days the following January, to be out of Portland for at least two weeks. She really wanted to go to Mexico, and I really wanted to make her happy, but I was uneasy about going, as a tourist, to where my grandmother had lived for all of her ninety years, where my mother was born and dreamed she, too, would return for a final resting place. I turned to look at Alex to see why he'd stopped cutting.

He squinted at his clippers and blew into them, sending hair into space like shiny, black dust. It was like I wasn't there.

"All right, lemme fade you in," he said without looking at me.

He didn't notice my silence, or he noticed but didn't mind. Maybe his resentment for people with money stemmed from dissatisfaction with his own inability to get out of El Valle. Living in Maine, I'd definitely met my fair share of people who identified with my birthplace by responding, "Oh, I vacation in

Arizona" or "My parents retired there" or, sometimes, "Jesus, what was it like being Mexican in a place like that?" The truth was, in my neighborhood, we stuck to our own. I didn't know I was a stranger in a strange land, really, until after high school. Desertwood High was mostly Mexican, so I became the sole ambassador for my kind once I went off for college in New England. Unlike my cousin, I did what was I supposed to, I got out of the hood.

Alex faded in both sides and the back. Then he touched it all up with a straight razor. Neither of us spoke. Once he sprayed the rest with water and started trimming the top with scissors, the clipper-less silence was too much for me and I had to break it.

"So," I said, already regretting that I'd chosen to speak, feeling like I was apologizing for my departure, absence and return all at once. "How're things around the hood?"

"You know. Same ol' shit," Alex said.

I waited for him to say more. He didn't. Part of me expected this, because I'd grown up with Alex, and he didn't say more than he had to—something I found annoying as hell at that moment. He knew I'd been gone, why wouldn't he help me out and fill me in? Make small talk? Anything? Instead, he kept snipping, with a subtle rhythm that I would've ignored except he also started beat-boxing as he snipped. I couldn't take it.

"Nothing ever changes around this fuckin' place, huh?"

This made him chuckle, I think.

He motioned for me to turn around so he could get all angles of my head. I couldn't be sure, but I felt as though he were mocking me. I felt like a child again, trying to pick fights with older kids in the hood, kids who always messed with me when I walked home from school by myself or when I turned down an invitation to play basketball in the park because I would rather stay home and read. Fuck them, all of them.

"But, hey, I guess that's kinda comforting, right?" I said. "I mean, it's cool to know I can always come home and not a goddamn thing will be different."

The snipping stopped.

Over my right shoulder, I thought I could feel Alex seething. Had I finally gotten to him? Did he realize that not all of us had the luxury of being dreamless? *Some of us* were compelled to get the hell out of our unknown hometowns. I knew early on that I didn't want to die in El Valle. Despite being born and raised here, I'd never felt like a native son. Nothing could be worse than being stuck somewhere you didn't feel like you belonged, and I knew it could happen to me, if I let it.

"You comin' to the party tonight?" Alex finally said from miles away.

"What?" I was sure I'd misheard.

Alex was looking at his phone. He'd stopped cutting to attend to his social life?

His eyes still on his phone, he said, "*Tío* Juan just texted me to make sure I bring my guitar tonight to the party out in *el campo*. You gonna be around for it?" he asked, looking up and smiling.

Blind-sided by my cousin's warmth, I'd have felt guilty if I wasn't so rapt by the odd details: guitar, bonfire, *el campo*.

"Y-You play the guitar?" I barely got the words out. I knew my mouth was wide open, I could feel hair clippings on my lips.

Alex laughed. "Yeah, dogg. I mean, I'm playin' guitar now 'cause *mi tío* ain't got no one else to strum, but you know ya boy can do things on drums, too," he said and mimed pounding bongos with his hands.

Then he sang in mock Pedro Infante, "*tocando mi guitarrita/ 'toy buscando una flaquita*," and strummed an invisible guitar with his right hand, and laughed. With each of his laughs I felt lighter, as though we were in our *tío's* backyard and cracking on a relative who wasn't present; the kind of laugh that used to float into the sky and take us with it.

Here we were. The cousin who'd been like a brother I never had, who taught me how to hop fences, how to steal candy from stores, how to look as good as a Mexican should to the world, the person I feared I would've become if I lost focus in high school. He stood in front of me, after so much time had passed and so little contact, and he was all right.

Was I?

Sweat on my face dragged bits of hair down my cheeks. Alex looked at me with promise.

"Y-yeah, I'll come," I said, finally.

"*¡Órale!*" Alex said. "Now lemme finish makin' you look fly. You know, it's mostly family there, but sometimes the *primas* invite their girlfriends. Mmm! Know what I'm saying?" He nudged me with the back of his hand and raised his eyebrows.

I laughed. I felt like I wanted to cry. Alex waited for me to stop and ran a comb through my hair like a blessing I wasn't sure I deserved.

"I'm just playin'," he said. "Your ma told me you got a girl already. She fine or what? When's she gonna roll through and meet the *familia*?"

I looked down at Alex's bathroom floor and saw months of growth scattered. I felt closer and further away from myself, like I was hearing an echo of my own voice after it bounced off some distant body and returned.

"Yeah, man. She's good." I sighed. "I'm not sure when I'm gonna bring her around but . . . wanna hear something kinda crazy? She didn't want me to wait till I was back home to cut my hair."

Alex banged his scissors against the comb—*tas-tas-tas*—and shook his head. "What? That's no good, dogg. People gotta let each other live, no? Good for you for doin' your thing, though. That's hella important."

He stood in front of me, combed my hair back one last time, like a painter putting final touches on a piece he might not see again. He stepped back and nodded with approval.

I tried to mirror his nod and his satisfaction back to him.

"I know you got a good handle on things, though," he said. "You always been the smart one outta all of us."

He turned away from me for the first time since he started the haircut. He knelt to open the cabinet beneath the sink and rummaged for a bit. He gave me a handheld mirror so I could see the sides and back of my head.

I took it but didn't look at myself because I wanted to listen to Alex.

"You think about shit for a while instead of just actin' on feeling," he said, looking away from me and towards the bathroom doorway like he was expecting someone. "Me? Shit, I just need to keep grindin'. *A ver qué pasa.*"

Alicia Returns *a la nada*

The last time my mother hit me, it was for blaspheming God in front of her.

I'll think about this to avoid thinking about how long I've been away from home. I'll have forgotten how sunny El Valle can be in the winter. The bright February sun will be the first of many cruel jokes. Coming back to the neighborhood will be another joke. I'll do my best to sneak into Mom's place without being noticed by any neighbors. But nothing happens here without everyone knowing, and *tías* and *tíos* will soon show up at the door. With too much food in covered, plastic bowls, too many apologies for my "losses," they'll let themselves in.

"¡Alicia, *m'ija!* We're so sorry about *tu mamá* but know she's with the *Virgencita*, now."

"Silvia was so lucky to have a daughter like you, *hermosa*."

"We wish it didn't take *this* to bring you home, but it's so good to see you, *querida*."

"This may not be the best time, *pero* when you get a chance, we should talk about some money things. *Nada serio*, you know, but it needs to be dealt with."

I'll be as cordial as I can for a bit, before I need them to get the hell out. "I need to clean up a bit," I'll say. "I need some time alone to think, to work, to call, to plan, to rest, to grieve."

At Mom's funeral, I'll stare at the horizon as though answers to my problems are off in the distance. The heavy sunshine will mix with the too-green grass, wafting sticky heat up to my face. Even though I haven't been to church since I had a choice, I'll recognize some of what the priest reads and recites in Spanish during the ceremony. Over the sound of my *tías* sobbing and my *tíos* clearing their throats in anticipation of the mosh of drink they will be consuming later, small pieces of the sermon will remind me of the last time I believed. I was eleven years old: sweat trailing mousse down my cheeks in syrupy trickles; my white dress clinging to my belly and armpits as I parroted *Santa Marías* and *Dios todopoderosos* in the stuffy, unventilated chapel. My mom afterwards had her make-up running because of tears and sweat, giving her dark half-moons under her eyes.

Maybe I should've known then, in the midst of wanting to believe but only being able to hear my own thoughts when I prayed, that it was never for me to become my mom's decent Mexican Catholic daughter-in-the-making. Maybe I should've known, when I was seventeen, that coming home past curfew from a party wouldn't be tolerated, no matter how self-assured I felt—a mixture of the gin I'd drank and the joy from earlier that night of a girl kissing me like she couldn't get enough. Definitely I should've had quicker reflexes when I told mom to "chill out, goddamn," as she scolded me in our kitchen.

Instead of fighting back, I went away and stayed with one girl or friend or another, only visiting every now and then. I didn't cry when she hit me, nor any of the other times we would fight after. I knew enough about my mom to know she'd been dealt a pretty shitty hand by her god, and I'll try to assure myself that she's going to meet him, because, I guess, that's what she would've wanted.

As they lower her body into the ground, I won't cry then, either. I'll rub sweat from my eyes, and the stinging salt and heat will make me think about my dad.

A few weeks after my confirmation, I went to spend my one weekend-a-month with him. He chain-smoked as we drove back to his apartment in Guadalupe from Jack-in-the-Box, and he hissed when I told him what was new with me.

"Confirmation?" He spat the words out like dirt on his tongue.

"*Mira*, Alicia . . . " he said. "Whatever your ma thinks you need to learn to be a good person is fine, *pero el problema es* that she *isn't* making a choice with this. She's letting someone else teach you *their* idea of good and evil."

I'll remember the way he took his eyes off the road for what felt like too long to make sure I was listening to him. He did this often, and it always scared me.

Looking me in the eyes and pointing at me with a cigarette between his fingers, he said, "All that *chingadera* are just words the *gabachos* use to keep us stupid and scared."

His truck felt as though it sped up the angrier he got, and the faster it went, the tighter my chest got. I nodded furiously so he could turn his attention back to the traffic on the road. Then I braced myself for him to tell me again about my *abuela* Fátima. She was actually my great-grandma, but Dad only ever called her *mi abuela* because she had raised him after my actual grandparents had succumbed to demons—their own and each other's.

As a girl, Fátima lost her entire family during Don Porfirio's war to exterminate the Yaquis. Forced from the only home she'd known, my *abuela* wandered north with other Yoeme, finding what could pass for refuge in the Arizona desert. We never knew each other, but she was alive in my dad's indignity and fury. He always evoked her spirit when he got worked up.

"*¡Una santa! ¡Una guerrera!* A survivor!" He would say. "A testament to everything *real mexicanos* should be, even after enduring all we have at the hands of invaders and crooks!" He clenched his fist, choking a smoldering cigarette.

When Mom's funeral ends, back at what I suppose is now my house, I'll accept everybody's condolences. A cousin will ask how I'm doing. We'll hug, and I'll say it's not too bad, at least Mom lived long enough to see me graduate and start my own life—all of which I wished my dad could've seen, too.

Then, I'll be seventeen again, pouring over essay prompts and interchangeable phrases from a five-year-old AP test prep book, Dad's apartment filled with the smell of Marlboro Red's and Fabuloso cleaner, a photo of Abuela Fátima watching over us from above the television.

"Can you believe these *putos gringos*?" My dad yelled at the TV—and, by proximity, me. "*Híjole*. They're really re-electing the *pinche* redneck from Texas?"

Sitting at the table behind him, I offered a "Yeah, Dad." I knew he wasn't really asking, he was only confirming his most cynical beliefs about fellow citizens, delighting in his own correct apocalyptic thinking, delivering closing arguments in his case against this country and the people who believe it is theirs.

"*A la fregada* with these fucking people!" He coughed out the last bits of this, like his anger and satisfaction weren't mixing well inside him.

I'll remember the way he couldn't control his cough, it grew more ferocious each time, like a wild bull gaining speed as it charged, and how I just kept reading the same passage from the workbook over and over again and not understanding the words. I wanted to get away from all of it.

Back at the house, a cousin will ask about my dad. Why, when he should have been talking to doctors about his health, did he leave? I'll remember the last time I heard my dad's voice. He had called my mom from somewhere in Sonora, maybe to ask her for help or to assure her he still didn't need any. By happenstance, I was also at her place, but I don't remember why anymore. When my mom asked if I wanted to talk to him while she took care of whatever she needed to do at that moment, I said okay.

"They think," my dad said over the phone, coughing, "they can poison me and then make me beg for help *como un nada de la nada!*"

Maybe it was because he was calling from some place I couldn't picture, but his voice came through warped and raspy, so I convinced myself I had no patience for the bad reception. Or maybe it was what the years—centuries?—of anger and pain had done to us that made me feel like I couldn't hear it anymore. I didn't know what I could say, so I only said, "Okay, Dad," and handed the phone to my mom.

That's when I'll feel it. Not a wounding, but an annihilation. Everything will escape my body at once. Everything will invade my body at once. I'll break, be ugly, wailing, alone: my own ghost and skeleton. I'll need nothing and everything. I'll tremble and heave. Somewhere across these deserts, my mom and dad will disappear, leaving me to hold myself, to be my only witness.

Arizona Boy

It all comes to an end, and I come back to Arizona.

"Ey, man, you know what? I say fuck that bitch," my cousin Hermes says about my ex-wife, Anna. "She ain't shit."

I can barely hear him over the roar of the wind against his pickup on the freeway.

I say, "Yup," and hope that's that. He and I haven't seen each other in years, and he's doing me a favor by giving me a ride from the airport, but I want so badly for him to change the subject.

"You already know how white girls be," he says. "They let all this therapy bullshit get in their heads, and then, 'You're the problem.' I seen some shit online about how divorce lawyers work with some counselors so they both make bank after people split."

I give another "yup" and think of Anna conspiring with a divorce lawyer to ruin me financially, and I almost make myself laugh. She's a financial consultant. I was an assistant manager at a bookstore in Newton. Any money she gained in our divorce would be like loose change found under a couch cushion.

Hermes won't let up. "*¡Pues órale!* Seba's back in A-Z, and a free man. We can hit up Mill or Downtown for chicks, if you want? The college kids ain't back in town yet, so the best drinking spots ain't hella crowded. Let's find you a fine-ass girl, huh?" He nudges me with the back of his hand.

"Yup."

I don't want to go out drinking with anyone. I want to drink, and I want everyone to go bother Anna instead. The Phoenix desert glides by outside my window, I realize I haven't seen my home state in nearly ten years. Hermes' laugh is annoying, but it also reminds me of a past life. I feel weirdly relaxed.

"How's Yessica?" I ask.

The truck hums softer as the excitement for drink and women gives way to the words of a pensive father. "Oh, man, she's great. Smart as hell, you know? I don't know where that came from 'cause I know I never liked school and her mom ain't much better," he says.

Rather than relate my own experience of being smart and brown and part of a family that had no idea what to do with me, I smile at my cousin and let him have his perplexed pride.

I snap out of it once I realize Hermes has driven past the exit for 101, which is the way to my parents' new place in Chandler.

"Whoa. Where you goin'?" I say.

"Chill."

"I want to go home, though."

"I said chill, fool. There's a party at Tía Sonia's house. Everybody's there, and they told me to bring you straight from the airport."

"Well, how come nobody asked me? Dude, I don't want to drive all the way out to Queen Creek. That's like an hour-and-a-half away." I can hear myself. I know I sound like a teenager, but this type of forced family bonding is part of why I left.

"Nah, homes," Hermes says. "See, the freeways all connect now. AZ's changed since you been gone. Shit's like a forty-minute drive now. We just gotta go around EV." He smiles, eyes on the road. "But it's all good with me if you wanna sleep. Your ma said you might be cranky and tired."

I want to ask what the hell else my mom said, but Hermes reaches into the small space in the bench seat and pulls out an energy drink. It'd be impossible to know the temperature of the can's contents, but the smell of high-octane sugar fills the cab the minute he pops the tab and lets the liquid gurgle down his throat.

"Hey, man," I say, my stomach clenching. "Can you crack your window or something? That shit you're drinkin' is making me sick."

He shrugs and opens his window. When I turn back to the road, coming at me are exits for El Valle and the Salt River Pima-Maricopa Indian Community. Then I remember Kino. I look over at Hermes again. Suddenly, neither one of us is thirty. We're not failed husbands. We're teenagers driving home one night, leaving the rez. I close my eyes, put my head against the window.

* * *

Kino didn't technically live on the rez, but he'd been born there. He lived just south of the Salt River Pima-Maricopa community with his mom and uncle. The rest of his family was still on the reservation, though, and Kino spent so much time there, he said he took the rez everywhere he went, like a rag he could use to wipe away any mess life gave him.

We met in second grade. Back at Polk Elementary, every O'odham, Piipaash and Diné boy was nicknamed "Frybread," "Big Frybread" or "Little Frybread." But even though Kino was Pima, I couldn't ever call him anything but Kino.

The first day of class, Mrs. Wright was seating us. We stood against the wall and waited for her to call our names and point to our place.

"Al-ar-con? Sebastian." My name left her mouth like a car struggling to start. I walked to my seat, trying not to make any noise or draw any attention to myself.

"Al-vare-rez. Kai-noh."

The skinny boy with black, black hair and ashy knees, grinning like he just farted and no one noticed, walked over and sat next to me.

"Mrs. Wright don't know how to say my name," he whispered excitedly.

"Yeah." I whispered back. "She don't know how to say my name, too."

In the seventh grade, our class had a field trip to the Phoenix Art Museum. I spent most of the day trying not to fall asleep while old white ladies with gray hair and gray sweaters talked about all the membership activities none of us could ever afford. Finally, after they were done, we were allowed to walk around the museum.

I looked at the paintings and tried to picture myself in them. I felt like I should've been born into a painting. Like maybe I was meant to be remembered as a kid instead of growing up to become some unknown adult. Kino, meanwhile, laughed at all the paintings—and there were plenty—of Indians. Some were of men standing around wearing animal hides. Others were of young warriors on horses looking determined and doomed. There was one with women sitting in a circle inside of a room, staring at the earth like it'd just delivered more bad news.

"I swear," he said, "you look at these and think that none of us ever smile without white people around." He walked away from me and into an empty wing of the museum.

"Well, what makes most Indians smile?" I said, after catching up to him. "I feel like I never see you not smiling, stinky-ass breath and all." I shoved him from behind.

He stumbled a bit. "Man, how the hell should I know?" He kept walking. "Probably a cooler full of beer or watching the Suns beat the Lakers, or, like, winning fifteen bucks from a scratcher's ticket." His hands were in the air, summoning the ideas. "That's usually the kinda thing that makes my uncles and cousins smile."

By this time, we'd made it out of the "Paintings of the Old West" wing and walked into wing called "Arizona in Painting."

Kino turned to me with his grin. "What about you? What kind of thing makes Mexicans smile and dance and sing those accordion songs y'all like so much?"

I felt my smile turn stern. What *did* make my family smile? What made *me* smile? I looked at Kino, his dark brown eyes fixed on me, and shrugged.

"Let's try to find some paintings with Mexicans in them and maybe we'll find out," I said, trying to be funny.

Kino turned and laughed. "There should be a painting of Amanda Smith. That would make you smile *real* big, *real* quick."

He took off running. I chased after him, my face hot. That son of bitch was talking too loud and Amanda was somewhere in the museum and could maybe hear him and then what?

He turned a corner, and, when I finally caught him, he was standing still. I grabbed onto his beefy arm and punched him. It was a pretty good hit, but he didn't react, probably didn't even feel it. He just kept looking straight ahead. I turned and saw the painting that had stopped him.

Staring at us, standing in front of dust, dirt and mountains shrunken in the distant background, was a boy. The mountains, the sky, the boy: all were grayish-brown like old wood or the moon. In a tattered hood and torn pants, he looked like he'd been carved out of stone himself, by thousands of years of wind, sand and sun. His hands were in front of his stomach. One hand held the other, as though he might attack if he let himself go. His face was pissed, calm and sad all at the same time.

Kino took a step towards the painting. Without thinking, I did, too. Side-by-side, we stood, so close that I felt heat from the back of Kino's hand on my own.

"Mr. Alarcon! Mr. Alvarez!"

We turned to see Mrs. Dunning. She had her arms crossed and looked at us like we were peeing in public. "What time did we say we'd all be meeting back in the lobby, gentlemen?"

We stayed quiet.

"It's almost 1:50. You two are lucky we didn't leave you here."

Kino snapped back into himself. "Sorry, Mrs. D. I was hoping to get a job here as a portrait model." He pulled at an imaginary bow and released, firing an imaginary arrow. "Mmm. Good hunt. Many buffalo. But still no smile," he said.

I laughed.

Mrs. Dunning didn't. "It's *that* kind of attitude that makes teachers not want to bring students here. If you can't appreciate these kinds of privileges, then why even bother coming?"

Kino's smile faded. His shoulders sank.

"Whenever you're ready, Geronimo" she said. "You, too, *moo-cha-cho*."

We ducked our heads and walked towards her. I turned one last time to look at the boy and the plaque next to his frame:

Eugene Berman
Arizona Boy, 1940
Gouache on Paper.

* * *

On the freeway, we pass the exit that would take us to our old high school, Desertwood. From where Kino lived, it was about an hour walk to Desertwood. He walked through nearly thirty minutes of desert: past shrubs, cacti, rocks and dirt. After those thirty minutes, though, the shrubs turned into broken glass, cacti traffic lights, rocks, cigarette butts and concrete. He stopped making this walk only when he stopped going to Desertwood.

I stare out the window of Hermes' truck, my stomach still gnarled. A loud *corrido* floods the cab. When the song is over, I take advantage.

"Hey, man, I thought you said I could sleep 'til we got to *tía's.*"

Hermes drains the rest of his drink into his throat, crushes the can and belches. "*Nel güey.*" He shakes his head. "Music helps keep me focused, dogg."

Out the window, billboards advertise a new casino that didn't exist in El Valle when I lived here. I feel a small, annoying pang of nostalgia. I tell myself it's just the carsickness and Anna. We'd visited my hometown once; she hated it. Once we pass the last advertisements for an outdoor mall, I turn to Hermes, who's tapping off-beat on the steering wheel.

"Hey, man," I say with nowhere else to turn. "You remember Kino?"

Hermes stops his tapping. He stares straight ahead, turns down the radio and sighs.

* * *

"Goddamn, dude. I swear, you look like Lawrence of Arabia crossing the fuckin' Nefud," I said and handed Kino the Gatorade I'd been drinking out of.

We met before school at a convenience store a block from Desertwood. For him it was on his way to school, for me it gave me a place to buy and smoke cigarettes, a habit I'd quit and un-quit for years. Even though it was almost October, or because it was still September, I was ready to get the hell out of Arizona's 100-degree days that never got any easier.

Kino, covered in sweat, took two big gulps of Gatorade, dropped his backpack and took off his shirt. His body glistened in the bright morning. He motioned two fingers towards his mouth. I reached into my pack of Marlboro 37s and handed one to him.

"You lucked out," I said. "It's my second-to-last one."

He used his shirt to wipe the sweat from his face, pulled a lighter out of his pocket and lit the cigarette between his teeth.

His smile came back. "Thank you, English," he said in a so-so Omar Sharif. "But you know I'd just hold your little ass down and take it from you, right?"

He flexed a bicep while he took a long drag. Abandoning the Sharif impression, he said, "Don't think you're all that just 'cause you found out you're in the top ten of our class." He pointed at me with the cigarette between his fingers and exhaled.

"You should try it," I said and threw my cigarette on the ground and stepped on it. "I'm saying, I know it's a pain in the ass to listen to all those bullshit presentations about college applications and financial aid, but it might be worth it. It'd get you outta here, you know?"

Cigarette back in his teeth, he looked at me like we both knew I was out of pocket. I tried to match his look: some weird game we played sometimes, like we both thought we had more to say but wouldn't tell each other. Then he shook his head and said, "What time is it?"

"7:20-something."

"Let's go."

"This early? Why?"

"'Cause, *ése*," he said in his growly Edward James Olmos. "There's AC inside the damn school, *vato*. *Wacha*, can't you see I'm sweating like fuckin' Moctezuma in the jungle, fool?"

We broke out laughing.

I lifted my head from my desk as soon as I felt the pecking. I hadn't been sleeping but I was out of it enough for Mr. Stapley to be pissed. The vein on his forehead bulged.

"You have *nothing* you could be working on?" he asked but didn't let me answer. "I don't give you free time so you can nap in class, okay? You're supposed to be using this time productively. College essays matter, I think *most* of your classmates would agree. But if you're going to be content with just doing nothing after you graduate, please tell me and maybe I'll let you have naptime. Does that sound like a fair compromise, Sebastian?"

The rest of my AP English class, even Kino, snickered. I felt my face boiling. I wanted to get up in Stapley's face and shove my transcript down his throat. *Ninth. You read that shit, Stapley? I'm ranked ninth in this stupid senior class. Top. Ten. Mother. Fucker.* I wanted to scream those words.

Instead, I said, "My bad, Mr. Stapley," and flipped open a notebook.

I pretended to scribble some bullshit until he walked away. I'd already written the essay I was going to send to colleges. A counselor had helped me put my story into words: my grandparents were Mexicans who came to the US just after the Second World War. My grandpa was originally a Bracero, a contracted migrant farmworker, and he managed to bring my grandma with him. Like both of my parents, I was born and raised in Arizona, a state where we were still foreigners. Worse for me, I was smart and got good grades and this made me more foreign as a Mexican. My life was pretty much written for me by others who told me where and why I didn't belong. I wanted out, if for no other reason than to find somewhere I did. Then I'd come back and throw it in everyone's face. Especially people like Mr. Stapley.

"Man, are you still butthurt?" Kino said and took a long drag from a cigarette and handed it back. It was after school. We walked to the bus stop to head to my place to watch TV or find another way to waste the day, the way I wanted most days to be wasted as a teenager.

"He didn't need to be an asshole about it," I said. I took a few small puffs and handed it back to Kino. I exhaled. "I'm not a loser going nowhere, you know? I mean, I can point to my grades and say 'See, I'm doing something right, so get outta my face.'"

Kino offered the cigarette again.

I waved it off and said, "It's all you. Kill it." As he took his last drags, I pressed him to back me up. "Let's get outta AZ, dude."

"You need to chill with that, I'm serious. You're starting to get on my nerves." He was still smiling, but it was the kind of smile he put on to get me to look away from him as quick as possible.

"What's it gonna hurt if you at least try, though?" I said. "Man, don't act like you're not smart or like you wouldn't be able to handle it. You're in some AP classes and I know your stubborn-ass likes books."

I put my arm around his shoulder, which wasn't easy since he was a solid half-foot taller than me, but I could feel his body rise and fall with his breath, and I felt like I could convince him if I lowered my voice.

"Let's get outta here," I said. To steady myself, I put my other hand on his chest. He let me, for a second.

But after a moment, he shrugged me off. "Hey, genius, you ever think not all of us hate it here as much as you do?"

His shrug made me stumble a little and I could feel myself getting hot. "You basically live on the rez, dude," I said. "And you're *always* bitching about how fucked up things are. The drunks, the junkies, the crazy-ass people. Why else would you be at a school like D-Wood except that you know you can't get anywhere with the schools closer to your house?"

I was still thinking about Mr. Stapley, about the people at school, about the people in the state: all of them fighting to keep me in El Valle. I was gonna fight back, Kino, too, if I had to.

"Man, you don't know shit about the rez, all right? Just fuckin' forget it," He shook his head, turned and walked in the opposite direction.

"Tell me I'm wrong then." I said, trailing farther and farther behind him.

He wouldn't turn around, so I got louder. "Tell me you want to spend the rest of your life living around this fuckin' shit." I could feel my voice become fragile, and I knew I couldn't say another word without it breaking.

We didn't talk again for weeks. In that time, I finalized some early applications to schools I knew hardly anything about except that they were in cities that were far away: Boston, New York, Philadelphia—all places I'd never visited. These places interested me mostly because they were big and cold and full of people who didn't know me.

At Desertwood, I'd still see Kino and he would see me, but we wouldn't talk. I wasn't mad at him, I don't think, but I felt like maybe he was mad at me and that made me feel like I needed to hold my ground. But I wished we would talk. I hated feeling alone. I told myself I'd be willing to cut a deal with Kino if it meant we could hang out again. I got my wish when he finally called my house one night.

"Hey, what're you up to?" he said, sounding very far away.

"Nothing. Procrastinating from homework."

"Ha. I figured." He paused. "Meet me near Hohokam Park on the bridge over the canal in like a half hour?"

"All right," I said, and we hung up. I suddenly imagined him all by himself in the middle of a dark desert. I shuddered.

Kino was calm at the park, smoke in one hand, beer in the other, but something about him still felt off. He was wearing a hoodie, despite the warm, semi-humid night. I sat down next to him, and he offered me a cig and a beer, too. We sat with our feet dangling over the stale smelling canal water. Neither one of us said anything for a while.

I finally broke the silence. "Was that you farting in Spanish class on Tuesday?"

"Hell nah!" he said and laughed. "I smelled something nasty, too. You know what? I bet you it was Brittany. I saw her and her friends getting lunch at Burrito Express that day. Whatever she ate wanted out in a bad way."

We both laughed.

"Shit, dude, that's too much." I wiped the tears from my eyes and took a sip of beer. It wasn't too cold, but it was cold enough. Just like nights in early November.

Then we both were silent. I looked down at our feet swinging closer to one another over the canal. The sounds of occasional cars faded into the sounds of crickets and the slowly flowing canal water. I turned to Kino. He was looking at me. He'd pulled down the hood from his sweatshirt. Light from the streetlamps lay gently on half of his face, making it glow while the other rested in a shadow. I wondered if he were trembling or if I were imagining it. Suddenly, he came closer. I heard myself take in a breath. I closed my eyes. I leaned into Kino's light. Our lips found eachother's quickly. Our hands caressed eachother's face. I breathed him in, smelling his cheek, his ear, his neck. Then I wanted to taste his sweat. I wanted to feel his heartbeat against me. To feel us harden on one another. As his hands pulled at my shoulders, I reached one hand to his hip and the other to his lap. I squeezed him, and he pulled himself to me.

We finished on each other. Laying in the grass, away from any light, I felt cold except the parts of me touching Kino. He lay on his back and I on my side, my head nestled into him. I could still taste him. He wrapped an arm around me. I reached my hand up to his bare, firm shoulder. Our chests rose and fell as we both fought to catch our breaths, our exhales powering the stars. Holy fuck, I remember thinking, holy fuck holy fuck holy fuck.

* * *

Off the road, on the shoulder, I wretch but nothing comes out. I know I'm not really sick.

"Put your finger down your throat, cuz," Hermes says from the driver's seat.

I ignore him.

Cars rumble past. I find an odd comfort in the thick, hot wind they pull behind them hitting me. I cough and spit and rinse my mouth with warm water from a bottle Hermes had in his truck.

When I get back in the cab, thankfully, Hermes takes me more seriously and doesn't turn on any music.

"We're still like twenty-five minutes away, if you wanna sleep, dogg," he says softly.

My stomach relaxes a little, but I still feel a thudding in my head.

"Thanks, man." I muster. I lean my head back and let out a deep breath.

"You know, I still think about him, too, man," Hermes says. He turns back to the road like the answer is still just out of sight. "Shit's crazy how people just go away, no?"

The thudding in my head intensifies. I close my eyes and lean my head against my window and hope for it to stop.

* * *

"That sounds like a shit-storm waiting to happen." I remember saying to Kino when he told me about Sky Washington's party. Sky's uncle was going to a funeral in Albuquerque, and since it was on the Sunday before Thanksgiving Break, he was going to be gone for that whole week. Sky's uncle had asked him to watch his house. Mostly, I worried because of Sky's reputation. He was an all right kid, no doubt, but the other rez kids would tell you that he was more than a little crazy. That Halloween, he had dressed up as a giant syringe and told everyone "I'm a huge prick" when they asked about his costume. A teacher finally sent him home, but only after a few others had tried and failed to hold back laughter. He wore that costume for the rest of the day, people who saw him after school told us. He even wore it to the mall a few days after Halloween. It was *his* party we were going to, on the rez—where you heard stories about crazy parties getting out of control and no official reports ever being filed by the cops because people just wouldn't talk about anything afterwards.

"What're you scared of?" Kino said. "I promise none of the scary Indians will want any trouble with a little Mexican kid, even if he is one of the biggest dorks in the school." He put his arm around my shoulder as we walked to class. The weather was no longer as hot. The further we went into our senior year, the less real it felt.

"So is his uncle cool with this? How the hell is that going to work?" I said.

I slowly moved myself from under Kino's arm. Things had been so much better between us. Since that night near Hohokam Park, we had found more nights to share. When I was with him, I forgot most of what made me angry or afraid. But afterwards I felt like I was doing something awful, not with Kino, but *to* him. I'd sent early decision applications to schools out East.

Meanwhile, at school Kino talked about cheap apartments in Tempe we could rent. We would live together, he said, while I went to Arizona State and he went to El Valle Community College. Then he'd transfer to ASU, so we could graduate together. I never told him I hadn't filled out any applications for ASU.

"Calm down, man. It's gonna be okay. You think I'll let anything happen to you?" He smiled, maybe thinking my nerves were because of the rez party.

I felt sick.

The party was worse and better than I thought. At least fifty people were there, pouring out of the mid-size house in the middle of the desert. Somehow, the music managed to overpower the collective clatter of talking, laughing and hollering.

"What the hell else are Indians supposed to do during Thanksgiving Break?" Kino shouted in my ear when he noticed how surprised I was to see so many people.

There were kids from Desertwood, older folks from the rez and people who looked like they didn't fit into either group. All of El Valle was there, it felt like. Everyone trying to shout over the heavy metal being blasted to the sky. Everyone drinking and smoking and dancing. Kino and I joined. Before too long, I had a heavy buzz.

Standing outside, behind the house, Kino was making me laugh. He had his hood pulled up over his face and was doing an awful impression of Alec Guinness as Obi Wan. When I stopped laughing, I saw his eyes, shaded by his hood, looking at me. He was smiling.

I don't know why, but I leaned into his ear, pulling his hood to the side and said, one last time, "Hey, man, I'm gonna end up going to Boston or New York. I got all my shit turned in. Save up, come with me."

He stepped away from me like something had bitten him. He hung his head, so that his hood covered his whole face. When he looked up at me, his mouth was stiff and he rubbed one fist nervously with his other hand, but he didn't move.

Feeling cold all of a sudden, I took a step toward him and tried to touch his shoulder, but he slapped my hand away. I tried again, and he slapped it away again and said, "Don't' fuckin' touch me."

I felt a spike go through my body.

"Hey, man," I said. "C'mon, let's go someplace where things could be better for us."

"Why don't you just shut the fuck up?" He stepped to me and pointed his finger to my chest. "What the fuck makes you think things will be any better for you around all those white people out there? You think I wanna be your lil' Indian sidekick on the East Coast? You think you're better than all of us?"

I could feel him trembling, and I wanted to make it stop. I tried, again, to put my hand on his shoulder, but he knocked it away.

"Don't fuckin' touch me, faggot!" he shouted and shoved me hard.

"Man, fuck all this!" I shouted and waved my arms in front of me.

What happened next is still a blur.

I felt his hands grab me. I struggled to try to land some shots on his body and to protect myself. I failed to do either. Kino dropped me flat on my back and I felt all the air leave my chest. He was on top of me instantly. Dark flashes hammered my face. I lifted my arms to cover myself after the fact. My head rang like a siren. I tasted blood.

I still don't know what stopped him. I don't know if he decided a few clean shots were. enough, or if people had taken pity on me and pulled him off before he could do more. Either way, Kino stopped and I lay there in the dirt, my body registering pain all over. Kino was gone.

When I finally got to my feet, I stumbled into the house to wash my face. I watched water drip in pink droplets from my hands, and I thought about how I had to say I was sorry to Kino. Even with my head throbbing, I knew I had fucked up. I wadded up some toilet paper and put it in my nose. In the mirror, I looked less like I got my ass kicked and more like I spent a day crying, but my stomach was churning, and my brain felt like it was pushing against my skull. I had to go home but I wanted to see Kino first.

I looked all over—in the backyard, down in the basement, throughout the house—but couldn't find him. I remember the burning panic in my temples, but I couldn't give up. I searched in front of the house and saw that Kino's mom's truck was gone. I froze. I stopped feeling any of the weight dragging at my body. Kino had been drinking as much as I had, and I was terrified.

Back in the house I tried to get anyone's attention, but everyone was too fucked up to do anything. Outside, I walked around aimlessly. Had no one noticed Kino had left? I saw a group of people standing around a campfire several yards away from the house. I recognized one of them immediately: it was my cousin Hermes. He was hanging out with friends of his who had graduated from Desertwood the year before. I ran over to them yelling, trying to explain what happened: Kino, his mom's truck, fighting, drinking, driving. Hermes, I remember, just kept saying "All right all right all right all right all right" and soon we were in his pick-up.

Surrounded by black and cold and wind, we raced down the road. I saw no trace of Kino. I touched the tips of my fingers to my swelling face. My lips kept drying, and every time I wet them I tasted blood. I don't remember Hermes saying anything. From that night I only remember the sound of the infinite dark wind against the truck.

Suddenly, the infinity was disrupted in the distance by flashing red and blue lights. As we got closer, I saw the squad car and Kino's mom's truck a few yards short of a well-lit intersection, where the rez met the freeway—the border between the Salt River Pima-Maricopa rez and El Valle. Dread tightened around my neck. I don't know how, but I kept breathing, kept trying to catch my breath. I could feel Hermes get tense. As we drove by, I fought the urge to stick my head out the window to try to see in the back of the squad car. I still regret not looking.

Days later, everyone in Stapley's English class was talking about how Kino wasn't coming back, that he was going to go live with some cousins on the reservation for a few months as part of a plea bargain. All of it felt too predictable, and I tried to tune it out. I told myself whatever had happened was a sign. What remained for me here? For months, in the halls, hushed voices surrounded me like a funeral procession. There was nothing left for me to do but leave.

Only in dreams would I see Kino again. In the hoodie he wore the last time we saw each other, he walks the impossible distance to Desertwood High, across all the years we've not spoken. He doesn't bother to wipe any of the sweat collecting on his eyebrows and on his cheeks. With my eyes closed, all I need is to extend my hand and put it on his shoulder. I do.

He turns around. Mad at first, he balls one hand into a fist and has to hold it with his other hand to keep from punching whoever just startled him. His face softens, though, when he sees who it is. Can he believe it? Can I? He pulls back his hood, drops his hands to his sides, and smiles.

I smile.

Neither of us speaks, but I want to tell him—tell us both—that things are all right. I want to tell him I'm sorry. It hasn't been easy, but we're okay and we're going to be okay. I want to tell him how during pitch black nights, when angry snow whips against the windows of my old apartment, I envy him and the love he has for his desert. (Our desert?) I want, most of all, to hear him say something—a laugh, an insult, a question about what else makes me think of him. His smile fades, he's about to speak, but Hermes shakes me awake and tells me we've arrived at the party.

Cero, AZ

Later that night, in downtown El Valle, after the reading in the bookstore-microbrewery in Phoenix where a barrio like his once stood, Cero lies on his stomach, his hands on his head, speaking only when commanded. The September afternoon heat, still rising from the sidewalk, claws and hisses at the exposed skin on his legs, chin and the undersides of his arms. Sweat coats him, stings his eyes, perfumes him in panic. He tries not to think. He tries to speak clearly and remain still. He punctuates all he says with "sir."

The officers don't ask for his name. They don't ask for anything. What they want to know of him is nothing. What they want him to know he cannot decipher.

Weapons drawn, they don't yell, but their commands batter him. Their words charging at Cero with malice.

Cero's pulse drums the concrete. He can't breathe. He fears he might never be allowed up to breathe again. Then one of the officers clamps down on him like history. His body spasms from instinct. Haunted thrashing.

* * *

"*¿Y tú, eres mexicano?*" Alejandro Zambra had asked Cero after he introduced himself at the bookstore-brewery and thanked him for his reading.

"*Ja. Sí,*" Cero said, excited to have the author sign his copy of *My Documents* and prompt him for further conversation.

"*¿De qué parte?*" The Chilean followed. "*¿Sabes que viví por un tiempo en México? Es decir, en el D. F.*"

Cero knew this. He had been a fan of Zambra's ever since a friend gifted him the author's latest collection of short fiction. Still, Cero laughed nervously. As always, the necessary clarification—the justification for his being.

"*Bueno,*" he said. "*Mis padres son de México. Yo aquí nací.*" He pointed down at the ground to emphasize "*aquí*"—on this land, in this country, everything it does and doesn't ensure.

"Ah. *¿Sí?*" Zambra said. "*Pero si hablas el español muy bien.*"

Cero laughed, still nervous. In twenty-plus years, he still had no template for these kinds of conversations, whether with friends, strangers, lovers or newly acquainted authors.

"*Gracias.*" Cero finally mustered, anticipating the author's loss of interest in him.

"*Y dime,*" Zambra said, surprising him, still. "*¿Eres escritor?*"

"*Sí,*" Cero said without thinking.

"*¿Qué escribes?*"

"*Poemas y cuentos.*"

"*¿Has publicado?*"

"*Sí,*" Cero said, but, again, compelled to clarify. "*Pero, sólo en inglés.*"

Zambra's eyes met his. A beat went by.

Cero scrambled. "*Pero me gustaría poder publicar en español,*" he said, nervously rubbing the back of his neck. "*Es que sólo soy capaz de escribir creativamente en inglés.*"

Zambra smiled, nodded, and said, "*Claro, pues, es tu idioma.*" He handed Cero back his book and offered his hand.

Cero took the book and the author's warm grasp.

"*Adelante con la escritura, amigo,*" Zambra said.

"*Muchas gracias.*"

"*Te cuidas.*"
"*Gracias. Igualmente.*"

* * *

On the burning sidewalk in downtown El Valle, a block from where the bus dropped him off, Cero's lungs stab against his chest. The cop's knee cleaves deeper into his back. He cannot speak. He has no language. He struggles only for the sake of doing so.

Then a consuming boom. A white devouring.

The Suicide Survivor's Guide to What's Next

A morbid streak runs through the whole of my family, but for you I could put it to rest.

—Vampire Weekend

Survive

Shaken, you wake up. Low hums of machines tell you that you made it. Damn.

Slowly you regain control of consciousness, and your new life becomes the smallest small talk with the nursing staff: How're you feeling today? Fine. Crazy weather for January. Yeah. You like Boston's chances come playoff time? They're one big move away from being legit. Anything else you need? Nah.

To questions from the hospital psychiatrist you hoped you'd never have to own up to: Were you intentionally trying to hurt yourself? Yeah. Were you trying to end your life? Yeah. Why? Not sure—stress, anxiety. Had you tried speaking to anyone about these feelings? No. Why? Figured it'd be a waste of time. Do you still think about ending your life? Not anymore. Why? Curious to see what Boston does at the trade deadline. Why did you try to take your own life? I didn't know what else to do. Do you still think about harming yourself? No. Why not? I'm not worth the trouble.

Don't think too much about anything or anyone, not even yourself. When you have an itch, scratch it and marvel at the fact that you're still feeling things like itches or soreness or numbness. Sometimes you wake up after your arm's been dangling off the edge of your bed and you appreciate each passing moment as feeling creeps back into you. The panic you thought would never leave you is gone. Or maybe it's just hiding; you're alive, so it must be alive, too, somewhere, right? But you feel completely empty, like a house whose tenants have been evicted overnight, so you don't think anything's alive except whatever makes you wake up in the morning.

You let the noise of the TV fill your room. You don't pay attention to what's on the screen, but it feels good to hear talk, especially Spanish.

A few days pass before someone from your pre-attempt-life comes to see you. It's Miranda, and she's pissed.

What in the actual fuck were you thinking? she says.

Somehow, she stops herself from getting in your face. You can tell from the stink of her breath and the oily sheen of her curly brown hair that she hasn't slept much. Her eyes are stained red and her face wrenches between confusion, vindication and longing.

You got nothing to say, so say nothing.

Miranda's the one who found you, according to the nurses. Defying your own expectations and probably some drunk-driving laws, she hauled ass from a New Year's Eve pub crawl in Portland, all the way back to Boston, after you sent her what you thought would be your final text, after you closed your eyes in your bed with alcohol washing down the poison you ingested. She must've used her spare key, the one you never took from her, to open your front door. She must've dragged you out into the cold before she called an ambulance. She must've been terrified and guilty and lost. In your hospital room, you're as stupid as the day you cheated on her.

Recall

Cinematic—yup, that's the word for it: cinematic—was the way you met Miranda. Good looking women are only supposed to drop an armful of papers and books in movies from the '80s, you thought. You'll be damned if that's not exactly how it went down. Worse still, it happened in an elevator.

You have a big enough imagination to believe it could've been some academic twist on a reality prank show: "Wacky Faculty" or something stupid like that. Otherwise, how do you happen to bump shoulders with this person, who, by the way, happens to be holding a copy of Daniel Alarcón's *City of Clowns?*

Are you reading this for fun or actually trying to give kids here some worthwhile books to read? you asked without any attempt at humor, handing the book to her.

What must your face have looked like? You weren't sleeping well then, because you had finally landed an academic gig. No small miracle for someone with only an MFA and one book of moderately selling short fiction. Still, rather than relax, you decided you were—instantly and perpetually—a candidate for dismissal. Not this time, you told yourself, and you spent the entire summer worrying and planning. By September you already needed a break.

She laughed, nervously, maybe even from embarrassment. But you didn't know then. All you knew was that her cheeks, flushed in crimson, came so close to her soft-brown eyes when she smiled that instantly you thought about what it might be like to nuzzle your face to hers.

No, she said finally. I mean, I've read it a bunch of times, and I'm *also* teaching it, but not until the Spring. For now, I'm still trying to get acclimated and do my best with the lit seminar classes. You know, trying to stay on top of it all.

You both remained crouched with your hands grabbing aimlessly at the papers all over the elevator floor. Your eyes locked. The fact that not a single person needed the elevator during any of this would add to your theory of reality-TV shenanigans, but it wasn't so. During that elevator trip up to the floor where your makeshift office awaited, for the first time in a while, you weren't convinced of anything at all. Things felt boundless, weightless.

I'm Miranda. She said her name like someone from your hood would've pronounced it; a barely noticeable *m*, long *e* sound, soft, barely-rolled *r* and *anda* like an elder shooing away kids. I'm the new professor in the lit department. She gave up the charade of collecting the mess and extended her hand.

You had to catch your breath before you felt ready. You looked at her hand and then her face, smiling between nerves and urgency. You grabbed it and felt your heartbeats sync, and your breaths flowed like the purr of the ascending car, and you smiled and introduced yourself, saying your name in Spanish like you hadn't done since leaving home.

* * *

So, explain to me how you're teaching Alarcón and Capó Crucet but it's *not* a Latino Lit class? you asked Miranda.

It turned out she didn't speak fluent Spanish but only because she was fourth generation. Her great-grandparents had fled their island right as the United States military invaded. Two generations passed before anyone considered returning, and that anyone was Miranda as a college junior. She ended up including some personal anecdotes in the preface to her undergrad Hispanic Lit thesis, which was available via research databases. You found this out through your online search skills. You wouldn't hear this from Miranda until later in your time together.

Standing at the door of her office, you were engaged in your new routine. You would "happen" to be on the floor where her office was. Your department head was also there, so it wasn't implausible. You ended up seeing more of him than he probably wanted. You were really there trying to maximize any time you might get with Miranda. Talking literature, lesson planning and university politics, you thought, was your way in.

Coming of age stories, Miranda said. We're also reading Jamaica Kincaid and Chaim Potok and maybe one more as soon as I get my crap in order.

She was always trying to do that. Whereas you looked at her office, and saw books arranged on a shelf in a way that could only signify perfect order, she was never satisfied. For her, perfection fell short of something better, something we just don't have the word for yet.

How are your classes going? she said, flipping open her laptop and typing like she was being timed.

Classes were fine. Part of the deal of bringing you in to teach undergrad fiction workshops was that you also had to teach freshman composition. The strange thing was, your two composition classes, each with twenty-five students, were prone to having more incisive and generally cool things to say about writing than your two fiction workshops, where aspiring authors had trouble challenging things.

You need to write through bareness before you can write anything fulfilling. An absence, a longing, a sense of without, *sin nada*. You don't write because you got something to say, you write because you got no other way. Frustrating but not surprising, your students, most of them sophomores trying on fiction like a hat in a store, did their best to write things that read like the stories they'd probably been assigned to read in their AP high school classes. They wrote because they wanted to assure one another that they were clever and probably also to show their parents that they were capable of doing "creative" things with their tuition money.

Classes are all right, I think, you said, dancing the words out with your neck. You tried to smile. Workshops are tricky, generally. Mostly, my approach is to remember the worst experiences I had in workshops as a student and then do whatever I can not to reproduce those kinds of shitty experiences for the kids, you know?

Miranda was quiet. She kept typing. You worried that maybe you'd blown your chances already. Were you too dismissive of pedagogy? Not dismissive enough? Either way, you were sure you'd said the wrong thing.

How are all your white kids taking the brown lady professor trying to push multicultural perspectives on them? you asked.

Her head perked up from her computer. She looked at you like you'd asked her to examine a rash on your ass. Still, she didn't say anything. Later, she would tell you that she likes to mull responses, like that one, rather than blurt out something first and then try to organize it afterwards, especially when talking to someone she was still getting to know and falling for. You didn't know this, so you stood there hoping for a blindfold and a cigarette.

She hmm'd, pursed her lips and fired back. They're fine.

Unfortunately, you weren't stricken dead. You were, however, sweating like you hadn't since moving to New England. Embarrassment bubbled inside you, and you wanted only for Miranda to finish you off quickly so you could go cry alone somewhere.

That's not how it went down, though. Instead, Miranda's face untightened, and she gave you a pitying look. You should've waited for her to say something more; you owed her that much in that moment. Instead, you said, I'm sorry. I'm a total *imbécil*.

She laughed. You fell.

Things between you got pretty good by the Spring semester. She taught her "Coming of Age Across Cultures" lit class twice a week, as well as her regular "Intro to Literary Studies" seminars. You kept the same amount of effort on your new composition classes, but the time you spent with Miranda was time you weren't spending on your workshops. It was all good, you were pretty sure. Occasionally, you'd oversleep because Miranda and you had stayed up late, making love and, in between, talking about where fiction was going, why your students weren't "inspired" and the pedagogical moth holes in your approach. Too often, you remember, the night ended with you telling Miranda she didn't know how creativity challenged the conventions of regular teaching styles—you'd throw the word "regular" like a pre-knockout punch. You'd insist that your students just didn't respond to openness, that they were too conditioned for dependence and, when you were especially insecure about her trying to help, you would tell her that maybe she should focus on churning out more PC twenty-somethings.

Then Spring semester ended and course evaluations came out.

Jeff, the head of the department, called you into his office the last week of May.

So, listen, he said, I don't wanna jump to any conclusions here, but can you explain why a lot of students in your workshops this semester said they felt like you weren't reading their work? His thinning white hair was like static on a screen and his trimmed white beard didn't move as he spoke.

You maintained eye contact with him the whole time. No matter what, you told yourself, don't look away. You didn't have any answers for him, but you hoped your quiet conviction would make him back down or do anything but keep you in his office asking you questions. No dice.

Listen, you know me, I think your writing is fantastic, he said and motioned with his hands to sell it. I mean, I love your book. Plus, you did a hell of a job with all the first-year comp students. He pounded his palm against his desk to emphasize "hell."

You felt, wanted to feel, like things were going to be all right. Maybe the kind words would shield you from what you knew was coming.

Wrong.

But, listen, the fact is, you're here to bolster the undergrad fiction program, and these evals are indicting, man, he said and shook his head.

The way "man" sounded leaving his mouth made you picture him when he was younger. When you first met, he mentioned that your stories, set in desert towns in Arizona, Northern Mexico and Southern California reminded him of his upbringing in Carson and his college days in Los Angeles. You could see him, his wild white hair more like the color of rust. Was he a surfer? Maybe a hippie, rolling doobies on the beach, listening to someone play guitar and sing half-baked lyrics. You wanted to kick it with that Jeff, or, at least, have *him* be the one telling you the bad news.

So, listen, I'm real sorry about this, Jeff said, bringing your mind back into his office, but Robert is going to take over the workshops in the Fall, and, depending on how that goes, probably the Spring, too. I'd really appreciate if you could take on two more comp sections, not just because I think you'd be good for it, but it's one of the only ways we can renew your contract for another year. Sound good?

You nodded like a stranger in a village where you didn't speak the language. You nodded fast and hoped Jeff would let you go. You wanted it to be over.

Sure thing, Jeff, you said. Sure.

Jeff insisted on keeping you just long enough to make it hurt special. Have a good summer, he said and stuck out his hand. And tell Miranda I say hello.

* * *

Of course you blamed her at least a little bit. Why didn't she tell you that you were fucking up? Why wasn't she on you about work? What was the deal between her and Jeff that you had to play messenger between them?

Some nights with Miranda made you swear all your previous diatribes to friends and colleagues and sometimes even students about the horseshit institution of monogamous matrimony was pure lip service. Some nights with Miranda, you two fell onto each other like snow on an empty street, harmonious, tender, inevitable. Some nights, though, you threw yourself against one another like storms at sea, like no one else in the world existed.

* * *

How could I ever doubt her feelings? You wonder in the hospital as Miranda sits crying, too far away for you to reach out and touch her. Life was never easy, but it didn't need to be. You would accuse Miranda of something, knowing she was already stressed about a billion other things, and you wouldn't apologize. Instead you'd leave her to find her way through her feelings, and you'd shame her for taking too long. When it felt as though she had unlocked a different part of you, a part you thought you'd left behind elsewhere, you needed someone to punish—students, friends, Miranda. Eventually, the only one left to punish was you.

* * *

In August, Boston still wasn't filled to capacity as most students hadn't returned for school. You sat in your apartment thinking about how you'd fucked up, and what was next.

Miranda had gone to Houston to present at a conference, but rather than make good on your repeated promises to look for a flight to join her, you stayed in Boston. The previous night you'd gone to a bar and got down with some woman you met. You told yourself it was stress or self-pity or just time for something new. You were turning thirty-one that fall, and you had convinced yourself that time was weighing on you.

* * *

When you think back on it, when Miranda stops crying long enough to look at you, lying in your hospital bed, you're unsure how to tell her how you feel about all she did. You can't believe she came back for you. Then you'll be honest about things for the first time since waking up. You love Miranda and you can't be with her because of everything you've put her through. No matter what comes next, you and she are through, and you're on your own.

* * *

After you cheated, you sent her a text—that's right, you fucking sent a fucking text—semi-confessing your sins. You weren't expecting anything other than a quick, short response with hell forthcoming.

Wrong.

Miranda called you immediately.

You didn't answer.

She called again.

You hit ignore again.

It was late at night for you, but her evening was just beginning.

Answer your fucking phone, she texted and called again.

You answered.

She was quiet at first. You tried to concentrate, tried to discern her breathing through the phone. She was crying. She became real again. You hadn't just hurt Miranda, you'd made her believe you weren't capable of this kind of cruelty and then you and your cruelty fucked just to humiliate her. As she gathered her thoughts to speak, you hung up and turned your phone off. It was inevitable, you thought, everything's gotta end sometime.

What if Miranda had given up that easily on New Year's Eve?

She came back to Boston a few days later. Her wounds had cauterized but not in time for her to make use of the rest of the conference or do a decent job presenting her paper.

You're fuckin' nothing, she said, a goddamn-piece-of-chicken-shit nothing.

She alternated between both phrases as she collected her things from your place. She moved with fierce purpose. Still, you followed her to her car, saying, I'm really sorry, over and over. You weren't looking for forgiveness, you just wanted an excuse to slink out from underneath your guilt.

She walked to the driver-side door of her car, opened it and stopped. She got quiet, and the sudden silence caught you by surprise. Was she going to laugh like she did once in her office? You took a step toward her, your arms starting to open in preparation for the weight of the coming catharsis. Miranda looked down. You took another step towards her, and just as you could feel the heat coming off her bare shoulders, she snapped her head up and spat in your face.

Just fucking disappear, she said. She got in her car, peeled out and sped off.

You told everyone at school you had plans to be on your own for New Year's.

* * *

You remember all of this, everything. Remember apologizing one last time in your text message. Remember telling her this was what you wanted, and you hoped her life could still be good and that she could still find someone. Remember thinking, around October, two months after the breakup, how you would end it all if you could work up to it. Your students, your days, your thoughts: none of it mattered. None of it relaxed the tightening in your chest. Remember what you wrote in a note by your presumed deathbed: "All dead men don't fall from the sky."

You say it out loud. A chill roars through your body. You shift uncomfortably in your bed. Miranda's tears slow down until she's breathing heavily and looking down.

You both stay like that. The moment grows, breathes. Then you hear the snort. You think you're hearing things, but then Miranda snorts again. A smile—real, painful, uncontrollable—takes hold of your face and you feel laughter coming like a speeding bus.

The two of you break like glass under pressure, crack then shatter.

You both know how corny it was of you to include that Alarcón line in your note, and there's nothing to do but laugh about it.

Present

You try to talk to her now. I'm sorr—

Don't, she says. She sits upright, keeps eye contact; she's not letting you off. Just don't, okay? Not right now.

Your self-pity heats into something angrier, and you can feel your heart beating like it hasn't done in days. What does she want from you? Is this about still trying to guilt you? Breathe. Whatever you do, breathe, but don't look away. She's not making you surrender in whatever game she's invented.

Restart.

All right, you say, you don't want any apologies, I get that. I get that. I do. Straighten up your back and you feel your chest puff out a bit. Eye contact, breathe. But I got nothing else right now. Shrug your shoulders and shake your head. You want an explanation? I don't know what to tell you. How about you pick your own adventure and you tell me?

Adrenaline kicks through you like a stampede. *Órale.*

Miranda doesn't give. She won't break eye contact. Her face is a mountain reaching beyond your sight, daring you to try to climb.

You'll take that challenge. Why not? A flurry in your blood. You want a medal? you say. Huh? You want me to tell you that I've been lying here, hoping for someone to come talk to me, to show I would've left some pain behind in my absence? (Easy, easy . . . the flurry's turning on itself.) And that I should've spoken up about my feelings? That I couldn't take work and the winter and my life? That I got too far to quit but I have no idea where to go next? The flurry is full-on tearing itself apart, and you can't stop it. Forget about comebacks or metaphors. Bury your face in your palms and weep. Let it out because it won't stay in.

Then you feel her hand, a reprieve you don't think you deserve, touch your shoulder.

Keep crying. This is just starting.

* * *

You're let go not long after. Miranda drives you home. You don't talk.

Boston didn't change while you were in the hospital: the grey sky and cold people paint a familiar, cartoonish, unwelcoming scene. Miranda reaches out a hand to your shoulder again when you get to your apartment. You turn to her, nod and try to smile. She squeezes your shoulder. You think you see a smirk flash across her face, but you can't be sure. You grab the small bag of clothes Miranda brought to your hospital room, open the door and walk up to your building.

Your basement studio apartment—admittedly, the nicest accommodations you've ever secured for yourself—looks like shit. The thought crosses your mind: it really looks like the previous tenant died and no one's been in the apartment since. Shake that thought. Quit thinking about death and get to cleaning.

Hum a song, beatbox without rhythm, just make noise. When you make noise, when you hear the noise you make, that's what keeps you focused on what comes next. Pick everything up off the floor and throw it into a hamper or trashcan, open the windows and let the near freezing air replace the stagnant past, make the bed . . . well, maybe leave the bed as is for a little bit longer. Lay low and build. Sift through the mail, the few cards sent by colleagues wishing you a recovery so allegorically, no one would ever know why you were hospitalized in the first place. Don't read them. Put them on your bookshelf. Make sure to text Miranda when you're sure she's made it back to her place.

Remember to close the windows when you're done cleaning, so you don't freeze when you're ready to try to rest again.

Go to at least to one support group meeting.

The guy who runs it, Phil is his name—you think, but it might be Bill—welcomes you as does everyone else. You feel all right, if not a bit silly, but this was your call. You don't have the money to see a therapist and you don't want the money to see a therapist.

First, the group prays. This catches you by surprise, but you roll with it. Next, people in the circle talk, one at a time. Everyone before you thanks god, or something like it, for getting them through their alcoholism or addiction or divorce or loss of their job or loss of loved ones. You know you can't stand up and leave, no matter how much you might want to, without sharing something in return. It might be a waste of time, but time is house money to you after surviving.

Stall, swallow a bit. I-I just got kinda overwhelmed by work, I guess, you say.

Smiles, concerned smiles, fill the faces of the other members. They nod, encouraging you to go on with your story.

You do.

I'm a writer, and I was, up until recently, an associate professor at a school across the river from here. You motion in some direction. You're trying your best to frame everything cryptically—no reason to tell these people too much. Besides, nobody said where they were from or got specific on when they first realized suicide was an option, or how it became their only option. The concerned smiles turn into concerned looks. This makes you go quiet. You scan the room looking for a smile to return, but none do.

You go on. I think I just had expectations...most of them probably self-imposed . . . pile on me . . . and they probably mixed with some other unresolved stuff I might have from growing up in a kinda rough place. You know, being a brown kid, having immigrant folks, the Border, and such.

Of the fifteen or so people there, most look like they've checked out, a few look confused, and Phil (or Bill) looks like there's an alarm going off that only he can hear.

After a few moments of silence, a short guy in a beige bomber jacket and a faded grey Red Sox cap lifts his hand but speaks up before you really acknowledge him. I don't mean to be rude or anything, he says. But what about writing got you stressed? And what's color got to do with any of this? Before you can answer, he keeps going. Now, teaching, I get. It can be pretty nuts. My sister's been a teacher with Cambridge Public Schools for twenty years, and I've seen her have to deal with bad administration and kids who only care about their sneakers and cellphones. *That's* a real stressor, I tell ya. Plus, you gotta watch yourself all the time now or some kid'll put some video of you on the internet and suddenly strangers are calling for you to be fired because of 'political correctness' or something.

As he gets animated, the others nod, and he takes their nodding as a sign of victory. You lose an argument you didn't know you were even having.

Y-yeah, you say and look from face to face for help. You're on your own. So, like, I don't really wanna get into "color," as you say, but I will say when you publish a book of fiction or poetry . . . (Motion for "book" with both your hands like you're talking to five-year-olds, instead of forty- or fifty-year-olds) . . . and that book brings you some attention . . . because the expectation for most works like that is that they'll only sell in niche markets . . . or, at best, friends of yours who also teach will use them as teaching materials so their classes will have to buy them . . . other than that, though, when you publish a book and it brings you some attention . . . you're, like, already behind on some sudden pressing deadline, you know? Like, suddenly you work for almost anybody who's read your work and you're also speaking for anybody who might look like you or come from where you come from. So . . .

Stop.

Who's this for? The people sitting in the foldable chairs in the community center's gym look like an audience forced to go to a reading for school credit. Even the guy whose sister is a resentful—probably racist—teacher has his arms crossed and is looking down at his shoes. You look to the group leader. His face hasn't changed, which is both impressive and fucked up.

You wrap up: Yeah, that's basically it. I was working too much.

Clasp your hands together. Sit there. Everyone readjusts in their chairs, stretches and whatever-the-fuck-his-name-is evokes the name of a higher force at work in all your doings and undoings. Others chime in. It's all white noise. At the bathroom break, get your stuff and leave.

* * *

You're not eating three square meals a day because your medical bills arrive in the mail and, since you're basically unemployed, you start looking for ways to cut expenses. You lie on your couch—because you still can't sleep in your bed—one afternoon, still smelling of last night's dreamless sleep. You think about all the funeral and medical costs around an unexpected death. If people who are thinking about killing themselves got their finances in order, to the umpteenth degree, you wonder, would society be more willing to let them go? Your stomach growls as your phone goes off. It's a text from Miranda.

How's the support group?

gave it up after one night. it was no good, you respond.

Ugh

i'm ok. I promise

Yeah, I know. You were "ok" before.

Your stomach growls again, warning you that you're not making good on your re-commitment to life.

Let me pay for you to see a professional?

You know you can't let her do that. More medical bills mean more investment in you from others and more possible losses on the gamble of your well-being. You're not going to let any more bets be placed.

i appreciate it, really, but i gotta figure this out for myself. i think maybe part of the problem is that i'm letting too many ppl i don't know try to tell me why i did what i did. thank you for everything. but i gotta figure this out my way. love you.

You put the phone face down on your chest and go back to staring at your ceiling. Will she text back? You know this isn't how a flame re-ignites, but you're not looking to start any fires. If your message is at all real, you're going to have to *do* things instead of *saying* you'll do them. You roll off your couch, stretch yourself out, put on a pair of sweats, put on your running shoes, grab your phone and leave your place.

Run. Just run. Push your legs until you can't. Breathe until your body hurts from breathing. Around corners, dodging traffic, down hills, up hills: run. Don't relent until you feel your insides smolder and you have to stop and retch. Don't worry about the people who walk around you while you're bent over. Besides, you haven't eaten all day so it's just bile.

You feel the crackling, frigid air replace the stale breath and emptiness inside you. Right then your phone goes off. Through blurry, cold eyes you read the message.

siempre <3

The walk back up the hill to your apartment is freezing. Maybe, you think to yourself, action needs a little bit of planning beforehand.

Move

Running, you learn through trial and error, is about balance. You have to go at the right time after you eat: too soon and you waste that meal because it ends up all over the sidewalk; too late and you don't go very long before your body yearns with hunger.

Each time you run, take a different route. Maybe answers can be found down an unknown street? You come home from running, sweating, sore and tired. Despite your body, you make lists and maps of different locales and neighborhoods: Green Street Café, Fernández Spa, Spanish-American Market, Roxbury House of Pizza, Jamaica Plain House of Pizza and, at least, three more Houses of Pizzas.

You were in the hospital for six days. Although you've been out for over a month, you still haven't figured out how to pay for those six days. You review the names of the places you've mapped while running. Could any of them be hiring? Is that really your next move, to go from writing to helping in a kitchen? You shake the thought and the self-criticism for the thought. Focus on a tangible next.

Do you need to clean your apartment?

You cleaned it yesterday.

Do you need anything from the store?

Not anything you can afford to buy.

Do you want to sit down and read something?

You look at your bookshelf and notice the stack of cards sent by well-wishers and pity-enablers. You haven't been back near campus since this all went down. You put on an overcoat, grab your phone, keys and wallet, and head for a train station.

The campus, wrapped around the Common, feels like a TV set. Just like you remember it. People cross the street one way, then the other; students interweave with the adults who are ahead of them in years and equally lost for purpose. You stand in the Common, observe as the scenes unfold, on a loop, before you take a deep breath and walk towards the faculty offices.

It's not until you're in an elevator with students that you realize you left your apartment without bathing, and, once all the students are off on the lower floors, you send a text to Miranda, as though being honest about how you smell might make it go away.

on campus. haven't showered today. hope you're in your office.

You exit the elevator on the twelfth floor and make a b-line for Miranda's office, putting your nose in your shirt collar to gauge your exact level of funk. It ain't good. At Miranda's you see through her half-opened door that she's talking with a student. You look up and down the hall and hope no one else sees you.

As if on cue, Roy, a media studies professor in his late forties, turns the corner and is walking your way. He's looking down and reading something. A few paces from you, he looks up and mutters a robotic 'scuse me, before looking again and realizing you're you.

Jesus, Roy says. He can't hide his—call it—surprise.

Neither you nor he says anything. You try, as casually as possible, to put your hands in your pockets and nod in the direction of Miranda's door.

Mouth still agape, Roy nods slowly and then grimaces a smile at you. You're sure he's close enough to smell you, so you offer your explanation.

Been running a lot, you say and pantomime pumping your arms and bouncing from one foot to the other. Good way to keep the ol' mind busy. You tap your temple with your finger.

Roy nods.

Finally, after a few beats he says, Mind if I get into my office? and points to your right with the paper he was reading.

Oh. Yeah, you say. Of course. My bad. You side-step and let him by.

Before he closes his door, he turns to you and says, You're looking all right. Keep going.

You nod.

You get into Miranda's office shortly thereafter. She looks beat.

I saw your text. I was worried when you didn't burst through the door, she says from the other side of her desk.

She lifts her glasses and rubs her eyes. You wait, out of respect, for her to refocus her vision before you say anything.

I gotta get outta Boston, you say.

She's silent at first. She looks at you anticipating obvious elaboration.

You haven't thought this all the way through, so you shrug and say, What else is there? I can't keep this up, I don't think. I need another start.

You weren't kidding about not showering, she says and frowns playfully.

You feel your body relax. You say, Plus, I got bills, and money that won't last very long here. I was thinking about going back to El Valle, you know? Reconnect with some family, be closer to where my mom is buried, save some money, get outta this cold.

Saying this aloud to another person feels like breathing truth into fiction. You believe what you say, and you let that belief carry your words to where they must go. Who knew faith could be so pragmatic?

That sounds all right, Miranda says. She yawns and stretches. You can sublet your place starting in March until the lease is up in September, yeah?

You nod.

Well, great. So, if you have any questions, go ahead and email me, otherwise I'll see you in class, she says and motions towards the door and smiles.

You laugh. Miranda's got teach-speak down and you're suddenly a little guilty that you haven't asked her about the happenings in her life.

So, I guess, for us this means . . . you start to say.

Miranda snorts and shakes her head.

Your face gets hot and you sense your body odor get worse.

You try to talk through it. Yeah, yeah, yeah. All right, I get it. I'm rusty on this whole 'talking-to-people' thing, okay? Cut me some slack, I've tried not to spend too much time in my own head, so my bad. Seriously, though, are we all right?

Miranda chortles through your rambling, but she calms down, smiles and catches you off guard. Nope, she says and shakes her head gently.

What's that supposed to mean?

It means we're not doing this, she says and rubs her eyes. It means we're exactly how you think we are. It means we aren't together, we're just getting each other through this.

Her voice is sturdy but not combative. She knew this moment was coming, didn't she? While you were cosplaying as a runner, Miranda figured things out. You're lucky to have ever dated her.

Her bluntness makes you uneasy, but your stomach growls, giving you an excuse to go.

I guess I'd better get something to eat. You offer her a weak smile.

Miranda is looking down at her desk and scribbling something on a sheet of paper.

Whatever, you think and stand up to head to the door.

Wait, she says behind you.

What? You sigh. What now?

You turn around and Miranda is holding out the piece of paper for you to take. She looks pleased. You walk back to her and take the piece of paper. You read:

Richie and Chase
writeorwrongpod@mail.com

You look back at Miranda and can't decide whether to ask a question or apologize for snapping at her.

She reads your mind and decides for you. No worries, you're hungry, she says. Anyway, this is a podcast a student told me about. A student, by the way, who's a fan of yours. She smiles. The hosts are two alums who run a small press in Somerville. They interview people, mostly writers. I haven't listened, and I probably never will, but it could be useful to you.

Responses like What? You're, my publicist now? or What the fuck's this supposed to mean? bounce against your jowls, but you breathe, nod silently.

Miranda senses your uneasiness. Email them, she says. You're a good writer and you still have stories to tell.

You shrug and say, Why're you pawning me off on these guys? 'Cause I shot down your pleas to see a shrink?

No, she says softly and takes a few steps closer to you.

You don't move.

She steps into you, puts her cheek against your chest and wraps her arms around you. It's because I think you need people to hear this story, and I can't be your whole audience—I never could.

You can feel her body rise and fall with each breath.

You put your hand on the back of her neck and rest your chin on her head.

I'm sorry I smell like ass, you say.

She snorts. *Me da igual.* I'm used to it.

Relent

Of course, don't email them right away. It might be true that you haven't got much going for you, but you're not chomping at the bit to talk to strangers about your newfound views on life. Plus, even if she was sincere and looking out for you, who the hell does Miranda think she is?

For a week, you continue running, barely eating and asking questions of no one. What? You're really going to reach out to random white guys in Somerville just because they have a halfway-interesting site and podcast. Yeah, you perused it a few times and listened to them review some recent fiction releases, so what? Honestly, will you let Miranda dictate some of your final decisions just because she's been nothing but supportive and caring, even though you've caused her almost nothing but grief for a year? Come on, are you going to send this email you've typed up, telling the guys you're around and would be willing to go on their podcast?

Your email gets a quick response, and before you know it, you're given a time and address for recording. Maybe if you weren't in such a hurry to try this whole "tell your story" thing again, you might've done more to dictate what you would and wouldn't want to talk about with them. You'll only think about this in hindsight.

The day of the recording, catch the trains you need to get to Somerville. The house where Write or Wrong Press publishes looks nice, even in the cloudy, Winter light. You knock and are greeted by two grinning, bearded, white guys. You don't know who's who, but they don't bother to introduce themselves, so try not to sweat it. They're excited to meet you and to get you on the podcast. You're not sure where the excitement stems from, but roll with it. They probably read your book, you conclude, and maybe some of your freelance stuff in blogs and lit mags. It isn't ego to think this, you convince yourself. The literary world in Boston is tiny, after all. Once pleasantries are exchanged one of them offers you a cup of cold brew coffee and it's off to the back room to record.

The recording starts and everything happens like a collision: in a flash and torturously slow. You learn that the redhead with long hair tied back in a bun and wearing thick-rimmed glasses is Chase. Richie's also got a standard Boston-guy beard, but his dark brown mop of hair is kept in check by a sky-blue Hyannis Port hat. They introduce you, give the standard bio saying where you're from and what your book's called. Then they ask you if you've brought anything to read, especially anything recent. You didn't, because you didn't know you were supposed to, and you also don't have anything recent. A small twinge of annoyance pinches the back of your head.

Sorry, I don't, you say.

It's just as well, Richie says. We figured today's recording might be pretty unique anyway. We heard through the grapevine that you recently experienced something kinda raw. Can you talk about it?

You stiffen. Your eyes go back and forth between both hosts. They smile with enthusiasm. You feel the dead air being recorded.

I'm not sure what you mean, you say, suddenly aware of your pulse in your ears. I mean, I guess . . .

Well, let me ask you this: how do you, as a writer deal with your inner demons? Richie ask. His voice takes on the character of a B-movie trailer voice-over.

First off, you say because you can't deal with this kind of arrogant inanity, don't cut me off when I'm trying to answer your goddamn question. And second, I'm not gonna feed fantasies about tormented artists or whatever. So how about you ask something else?

A silence re-takes the room, filters into your mics and meets your ears.

All right, Richie finally says. His voice wavers at first but then steadies. Can you talk about your life in the past few months?

How the hell did they learn about your almost-suicide? You wonder. Miranda? Her student? Are you really going to open up to two complete strangers on a recording? You don't have too much time to think, so take a deep breath and talk.

So, yeah, you say. I went through something kinda . . . rough recently, but probably not for the reasons you wanna hear.

Both hosts lean eagerly over the table. You would stop, but you have to admit, something about their attentiveness makes you feel strangely in control.

Honestly, I was in a support group meeting-thing recently, and my biggest take-away was y'all don't really know and can't really know what I've been through. And you know what? *I* may not even know what I've been through. Pause. Take another deep breath, let it out. My family or friends back home may be the only ones who could possibly know what I'm experiencing . . . and I can't really ask most of them because some aren't with us anymore . . . and the ones who are, I haven't talked to since I left.

You close your eyes and try to dwell in your own revelation. You don't care how much silence fills the room. You take your time, forgetting there's anyone else around. Open your eyes but look only at what's right in front of you. Start again. Now that I'm talking, I'm remembering a lot about my own history, how my life stacks up against the lives of people who came before me, you say and pause. Like my maternal grandfather. He died before I was born, but everyone in my family swore I looked just like him. You get weird spiritual inheritances like that in Mexican families, and . . .

Like reincarnation? Richie says.

Yo! You snap. What'd I say about cutting me off? This is a story, all right? Stories gotta have time to build.

He offers you an apologetic look.

Anyway, you say, I only ever saw pictures of my grandpa, and I didn't really appreciate our resemblance until my mom guilted me into travelling with her to her hometown in Mexico when I was seventeen. I hadn't been since I was a little kid because my grandmother had died a few years prior . . . so our reasons for visiting were limited to when my mom felt like going.

You notice Chase's eyes starting to wander. Ignore him. You're no one's suffer-porn performer. This is for you. Your story. Continue with it: On this trip, I walked to the store once while my mom took a nap.

It was near dusk, it had rained for most of that day and I hadn't roamed the streets of my grandparents' *colonia*, their neighborhood, since I was like six or seven, so I wanted to take the opportunity to do so without my mom . . . you know, just kinda restless and feeling like surveying the landscape after a storm.

Remember when you walked around and expected to find something familiar, as though the lay of the *colonia* could come naturally to you, like it was preprogrammed in your mind.

So, I round the corner coming back from a store, and there's this old man sitting in a *mecedora*—erh, rocking chair—and a woman, probably his wife, sitting in the rocking chair next to him. Maybe I'd met them as a kid, but I didn't remember. Anyway, they saw me and then their eyes got wide. Their faces white. To them, my grandpa had come back from nowhere to haunt the *colonia* again. I'm seventeen, right? And I'm in a pair of shorts and a T-shirt. I was born and raised on the other side of the border, but that interaction was meant to remind me of something bigger. It was like something I'd inherited was finally returned to where it belonged.

The two guys nod along. Keep going.

Even though my grandpa and I never walked this earth at the same time, we sorta shared this space years apart. I felt really at home there, miles away from where I was actually born. It's like this interaction was already written on this place and I was reading it on the land. So, I tried to capture and appreciate these kinds of inheritances and experiences in my daily life and in my writing, you know? That's pretty much how my book of short stories happened. . . . It's sorta how I still see things, or at least, how I think I *should* see them . . . if ever I wanna recalibrate my mind.

Both guys nod. After a moment Richie asks, wait. So how's this relate to your struggles?

Chase—not the thinker of the two—suddenly also isn't satisfied. Yeah, he says like you're pulling a fast one.

You think about it, but shake your head. You know there wasn't ever an escape from this, no easy way home. Still, what's yours is yours.

I don't know, man, you say. I don't think I was trying to undo myself of anything. I think about my family and how, at different times, they gave of themselves to get me here. . . . And now I'm here. And maybe I need to figure out what's worth giving up to keep going. It's these exchanges that are weighing on me now. I think too many of us here have been giving more of ourselves than we can ever get back. Eventually, we're less than anything we trade for. Then what? Maybe there's something to getting to choose when we don't want to trade what's left for anything else. Maybe we start to keep more of ourselves from the world.

So, what's next? Chase says.

You smile. They don't. Next? You chuckle. I get the hell outta here, maybe for good.

You take off your headphones and put your microphone down.

Don't bother me with anything else, you say over your shoulder as you exit the room.

Neither of them follows you.

Still, you keep talking. Not all answers fall from the sky, y'all.

Outside, walking to the train station, examine things in the dimming daylight. Breathe it in gently. In the empty streets, silence wraps around you. Take a moment, imagine all of this without you here. Try to convince yourself you notice a difference.